KILLING ROSIE

SUZI WIELAND

Copyright ©2019 by Suzi Wieland
All rights reserved. The reproduction or utilization of this work in whole or in part, by any means, is forbidden without written permission from the author.
This book is a work of fiction. Names, characters, places, and incidents are products of the author's imagination or are used fictitiously. Any resemblance to actual events, locations, or persons, living or dead is entirely coincidental.
Published by Twisted Path Press
Cover by Krafigs Design
First edition March 2019, Second edition July 2024

Chapter One

Ten days 'til Rosie dies

The shrill voices drive into Lawson's head like nails in a coffin, the stuffy windowless room bearing down on him. Air... he needs air, but he also needs to finish with these two twits. Then fresh air and maybe a drink.

"I don't know why you get to decide everything. You always do this to me, just because you're older. It's four minutes for heaven's sake." Stina. No Linn—no, he's not even sure which woman it is—flips her hand in the air to brush off her twin's comment, turning her pert nose and flashing her indignant baby blues.

"No, Stina. I'm the one who should decide how she dies. I'm the one who has to take the brunt of her..." Linn stares at him for a few moments, tears building in the same blue eyes lined with too much black makeup. "I'm the one who has to protect our little sister all the time from her. She hurt me badly, Mr. Wolf. She always does." Linn's gaze drops to the table, and she sniffs long and hard.

"What?" Stina's voice rises an octave. "That's not true. She's worse on me."

Law clenches the pencil in his hand, wanting to tear his black hair out strand by strand. No, better yet, all the hair on the heads of the two bickering bitches in front of him. With the dough from these over-privileged twits, he'll be able to head up sooner to that farmland in Stilla… a long, long way from the likes of these two and every other crackpot he's had to deal with in his line of work.

He tosses his pencil down, and it rolls across the scarred cherrywood desk. The movement doesn't grab their attention.

"Ladies," he says, using the term loosely, "typically we discuss other things before we talk about the method of death. Time is money, and my rates will start rising soon. So tell me more about your sister and why she deserves to die."

These two barely sat in their seats before they started planning their sister's death, but he hasn't even had a chance to determine if their sister, this Rosie, is someone who doesn't deserve to live.

"She's awful, Mr. Wolf." Stina slumps in her chair and peers up him from under her lashes. "When we're not home, and when Mother's not there, Rosie invites men into our home for…" She glances at her sister. "Sex," she says softly. Her face burns bright red.

"That's not a crime."

"That's not what she means," Linn pipes up, fingering the buttons on the top of her long-sleeved shirt. "She's a lady of the evening."

"A prostitute?" Law asks.

"Yes." Stina sighs as if they've been trying to get him to understand for hours. "She sells her body for sex and has these strange men in our house, and she's made our sister do it."

"Wait, what?" Law sits straighter. Now the story has become more interesting.

"You don't know Rosie," Linn continues. "All she cares about is money, and she started making our sister do it too. She's only fourteen."

Law cringes on the inside, but he doesn't show the women his true feelings. He's learned over the years to hide his emotions deep inside.

"Why haven't you talked to the sheriff?" he asks. Their embroidered shirts, long skirts, and leather boots are those of women with money, but not enough to throw it away on anything. Most of the women who end up prostituting themselves do it because they have no choice. They're not usually women from the class these two belong in.

KILLING ROSIE

Linn throws her hands in the air. "Because he's in on it. He comes to the house too." She babbles on about how scared she is that he might discover they know of his illicit games.

Not a surprise. So many in the sheriff's department are corrupt, and a lot of the judges can be bought off. There are honest men in the system, but the crooked ones keep the bad guys on the streets, even when it's plain as day they are guilty. If the system was fair and just, then Law wouldn't have a job.

"But, Linn, tell him about what Rosie is doing." Sister and sister stare at each other. Their faces are the same, but their clothes and hair are different.

"She hits us if we don't do what she says, and she broke Mother's arm last year. And I just found out that she's bringing our sister here to Staden to make her work at Nova's Favor. To teach her the ways of the working girls. Then she's bringing her to Radda to start up her own place."

Law's mouth drops, and he quickly closes it. Nova's Favor is the nastiest brothel in town. He rescued a sister of a former client from there once when her boyfriend sold her off. The guys who run the place have no qualms about kicking the crap out of some poor woman and then making her service men. The building is in the worst part of town, hidden behind a sketchy bar. No way they would know about Nova's Favor on their own, not these prissy gals.

"I'll do it," he says with conviction. "We need to save your sister."

The thought of this Rosie forcing her fourteen-year-old sister into a place like Nova's Favor turns his stomach. Women who *work* there leave broken and destitute, shells of the people they used to be. No woman should be subjected to a place like Nova's Favor.

"Oh, Mr. Wolf, thank you." Stina bats her lashes at him. "May I have a glass of water? My throat is parched."

Has she forgotten where she is? Law tempers his smile. "I'm sorry. This building, like most others in the neighborhood, have no indoor plumbing." The area is too old and poor to have been such a luxury. "There is an outhouse out back if you need one though. And a well not far away."

"Oh." Stina shows her disgust. "Never mind."

Over the next half hour, he explains how things will work. Rosie definitely deserves to die, but Linn and Stina argue over almost every minor detail, making him want to kill them. Law just wants his payment and to get the job done quick and easy, and then he can go on his merry way.

KILLING ROSIE

Finally, they arrive back at the method of death. Some of his clients are set on what they want done; others don't care and just want the person gone. All these targets deserve painful deaths, but Law prefers the non-messy ones where he can get in and out.

"Stina, you're being difficult." Prissy missy slaps her shiny red nails on her hips and scowls at her twin sister.

"No, Linn, you are. You know Mother can't stand the sight of blood." Stina whips her head back to Law, her blonde hair flying through the air. "Strangle her. Mother will rave if you spill blood on the wood floors."

"Yeah, okay. No blood. So after you give me the payment, I'll take care of Rosie."

Condemning a fourteen-year-old to work in a brothel is shameful, horrendous, and he has to save the poor girl from her so-called sister Rosie.

Linn pulls out a wad of cash and hands it to him. "It's been so nice to work with you, Mr. Wolf. Thank you."

Stina grasps his hand to shake but doesn't let go. Her black-caked eyes flutter up at him, and she speaks in a throaty voice. "Perhaps sometime we could meet for pleasure, instead of business."

Law keeps the laugh from his face. She can't be for real. He drags his hand back gently and forces a smile. "If I wasn't married," he says, winking.

The sisters are about five years younger than him, perhaps twenty years old, and are both stunning beauties, but dating a customer is only trouble—not that he's interested in her anyway.

"Where's your ring?" Linn crosses her arms and glares at his hand.

"In this business, it's very important to remain anonymous, and my wife prefers I not wear it." He's used the wife excuse before, although he's never been married.

The two sisters seem to accept his answer.

Law ushers the two women to the door of the temporary office. A permanent office would make it too easy for the sheriff to trace back to him.

Although he rarely gets any satisfaction out of his jobs, this one might come close. The things Rosie has done to her little sister… she definitely deserves to die.

He counts the bills a second time, excited to go home and hide his new stash. He refuses to use banks, and since he's been saving his earnings, he's got a lot of cash locked in several safes.

All he wants is to go home and clean up, and then it's time to celebrate.

KILLING ROSIE

Law slides into his favorite spot at his favorite establishment, the perfect place to blow some dough. Loud music plays in the dim room as sexy lingerie-clad women scrounge the floor for suckers, but he's not one, at least not for all those dancers.

He's only a sucker for one gal—Sunny Daze—the woman who keeps him coming back every week, and one of the few people he'll miss once he moves away from Staden.

"Hey, handsome." A raven-haired beauty with big boobs lays her arm around his shoulder. Obviously a new girl because most of the regulars know he belongs to Sunny. He doesn't mind Raven's round melons pressing into him though.

"I'm looking for Sunny." He scans the floor for his auburn beauty but doesn't see her.

"Ahh." Raven pouts. "Are you sure? Maybe you'd like a dance from me because I'm—"

Smack. One of Sunny's friends struts away after giving the girl a swipe on the head.

Raven frowns, backing up a few steps. "I think she's on break. I'll let her know she's got a visitor if I see her."

Yeah—doubt that'll happen. Law can wait though, and he settles back with his beer to watch the sweet girlies dancing on the stage. They don't get completely naked here, but a little mystery is preferable.

Ten minutes later, lean arms wrap around his shoulders, and he drinks in the flowered scent of Sunny.

"Hey there, Law, heard you were looking for some company." Her sultry voice drills into his ears, getting him all excited. He's not dumb. He knows it's all an act—she's a dancing girl out to earn money just like the rest of them, but for their short time together, he likes to imagine it's all about him.

"Just waiting for you, doll." His heart picks up speed with her hot breath on his ear, but she releases him and trails her finger down his arm as she parades around the side of his chair. Her thick auburn curls spill over her shoulders, and she adjusts the long cape, black velvet on the outside and silky red on the inside so that Law can take in her whole body.

She's always in the cape with the black bustier, propping up her luscious boobs. A tiny bit of exposed skin shows, and then it's the black panties, lace stockings, and knee-high boots.

Law jumps out of his seat to pull back her chair.

"Thank you, kind sir." Her smile and gratitude are real. Most assholes think that because these women are dancing girls, they can treat them like dirt.

Not Law.

"Great timing. I'm free, so you got me for the next half hour." She sits and gives him that seductive smile that drives Law wild, and he slides over a glass of her favorite white wine, which gains him another thank you. "So talk or dance first?" Sunny cups his stubbly chin, running her finger along the side of his jaw.

"Maybe a quick dance."

Sunny isn't like some of the other girls. She doesn't reveal much about her personal life, and she's smart, has her own opinions. She doesn't become a yes-woman just to make another buck off Law.

He scoots closer to her, their arms touching on the table. Tonight will be the last dance from her because he doesn't plan on returning to the city for a long time.

Her mischievous smile and sparkling eyes rev him up, and she stands in front of him, sweeping her thick hair off her neck and arching her back. Her hips rotate to the beat, and he clenches his hands to keep from placing them on her curvy hips. Touching is not allowed at this establishment.

Beautiful women shake their asses for men all around him, but Sunny is the only one he wants to watch. Her body continues to sway, even as she lifts her leg and rests her boot on his chair.

He wills that tiny piece of fabric covering her crotch to slide over, but her panties refuse to show him her goods. She grins, knowing exactly what he's thinking.

"Just one peek," he begs.

"Not going to happen." She laughs. Every week he asks her the same question. That cape would keep anyone from seeing the improper move, but she never does. And he likes that about her.

Instead she spins around and tugs the cape so it's hanging down her front. She backs into him, her ass shaking. Closer and closer. Law wipes the sweat off his forehead.

He's hard—she always does that to him, but after her dance, when they talk, will give him time to retreat. He draws in a deep breath to slow his beating heart and takes a drink to cool off.

The song ends, and Sunny perches in her chair and sips on the Chardonnay. He's jealous of that wine glass and how her pouty red lips caress it.

"Why is it you always look like you're the one working out when I'm the one dancing, and you're sitting?" Sunny laughs, and Law joins in.

"I put my time in earlier," he says. "All done now."

KILLING ROSIE

"How was your day?" she asks.

"Just the usual. Ornery clients." He chuckles. She thinks he's a salesman, and so they share the common bond of working with demanding customers. It's funny how their relationship is balanced. She has secrets, not that he can blame her for keeping her personal life out of the lounge, and he... well, he can't exactly tell her he's a paid assassin. Of course that's only until this last job is completed. Then he's done.

Forever.

"Got some news," Law says.

"What's that? You win the lottery?" She winks. He'd never gamble his money away, and she knows it. Sunny Daze is his one and only vice.

"Nope. Actually, I'm retiring. Getting a new job."

"Good for you. I hope it's something you'll enjoy. One day I'll have a job like that. A job I love." Her brows close in, and the smile falls from her face. She's talked about her dream of working in a flower shop, saving her money until she can start her own store. "Then maybe I won't have to take on another job."

"Another?" He tilts his head, studying her face. She already spends her mornings working as a maid.

She looks surprised as if she hadn't meant to say anything. "It's temporary. I'm just helping a friend next month with some sewing for her shop." She pats Law's hand, her eyes wide. "What about you though? What will you be doing?"

He doesn't want to admit the truth. Most people look at him like he's crazy for wanting to move away from Staden and start farming.

"Not quite sure yet, but I'm moving to Stilla."

Her eyes pop open, and she leans in closer. "You're moving to the country?"

"Yes. I'm ready for a change of pace." Working the soil, working with his hands, creating life instead of taking it away.

"That sounds wonderful, really." Sunny lays her warm hand on his arm, giving him a wistful smile. "But I'll miss you."

The truth. He can tell.

"I'll miss you too. It's been fun." And then some. Every night Law leaves the lounge, he returns home to imagine making love to Sunny. Even when he bangs other girls, he pretends they are Sunny.

"You know what…" Sunny's hand remains still, a deepening blush on her face as she stares at the table.

Law leans over and whispers into her ear. "What?" He's never seen her embarrassed before.

"Well, um… normally I don't do this with customers, but since you're leaving town, maybe I can give you a special goodbye." She reaches under the table and squeezes his thigh. "I've thought about what it'd be like to be with you, and I just can't let you go without finding out."

Law's tongue freezes in his mouth.

The guy whose nerves never fray, even when he's about to end someone's life, now feels like a teenager on a first date. He swallows a few times so that his voice doesn't come out all croaky.

"If I'd known that, I would've moved away a long time ago." He runs his lips across her ear, and she shivers. "In other words... yes," he adds.

Her smile fans the flame inside his body, and she slowly leads him back towards the private rooms. He stares at the back of her red head, almost level with his. Those long legs must put her at about six feet, just a few inches shorter than him.

At the entryway to the hall, some guy stands there trying to be all imposing, but he doesn't scare Law. He's just there to cut down on the hanky panky. Sunny whispers into his ear, and he nods, then she slips something into his back pocket.

Law follows her down the hallway of slightly open doors—required by lounge policy. At the end of the hall, she opens the door to a room he's never been in. Spending money on private dances is not his thing, and no way he's gonna pay to bang some girl when he can find willing ones almost anywhere.

The tiny room holds a settee and nothing more than a few candles along the wall. Mood lighting.

Law wants to whip Sunny around, rip off her clothes, and screw her till she screams, but this is her show, so he'll defer to her wishes.

She nudges him onto the cushions and kneels in front of him. All he can see are those luscious melons, waiting to be touched. Her fingers deftly unbutton his trousers, and he raises his ass so she can remove them. Grasping his underwear, she gives him a sly smirk.

"So will I have to coax the big guy out, or will he come out on his own?" Her raspy voice sends that fire coursing through him, and while she stares at his manhood, it magically rises. "That's what I thought." Sunny winks at him and yanks down his underwear.

Someone raps on the door, and neither of them moves an inch.

A hoarse voice yells as the doorknob shakes. "Get this door open, Sunny."

Her pale face grows even whiter, and she shoots to her feet. "Get dressed. Now," she hisses. "Just a second, Grier. The door is stuck."

Law pulls his underwear and trousers up, buttoning them in record time, then he slides a hand through his black hair, although it's so short it probably isn't mussed up.

"Don't pull that crap with me. Open this damn door." Grier pounds again.

Sunny glances over at Law, then reaches for the door. Law sits his ass on the settee and waits for the storm to blow in. She wraps the cape around her tightly and opens the door. It whacks into the wall, and a big bruiser with an angry face stalks inside the room. He does a once over on Sunny, then checks out a smirking Law. Arms crossed, he turns back to Sunny and snarls. "What the hell, Sunny. You know we've been having problems with the other girls. And now you?"

Sunny drops her head and bites her lip. "I'm sorry, Grier. It's just that, well… Law surprised me tonight. We've been together for three months. It's our anniversary, and I just thought… we just wanted to… I'm sorry."

"I don't give a damn about your boyfriend. Pratt's trying to keep this place clean, and it's my ass when we have problems. You can screw him at home, but when you're at work, you stick to the rules. Got it?"

Her head bobs. "I'm sorry. It won't happen again."

Grier's gaze drills into her and Law, then he turns for the door. "If I see this door closed again, you're out of here."

"It won't. I promise."

Grier stomps away.

She returns to Law, her head hanging. "I'm really sorry, Law. I shouldn't have… We shouldn't have. Mr. Pratt is a decent guy, and he's really trying hard to keep this place respectable. And it's just they've been having problems with some girls. Obviously Fallon—he's the guy who was at the door when we came, he looks the other way, but Grier. He just—"

Law sticks a finger to her lips to shush her. "Don't worry about it. I'm sorry I got you in trouble." She needs this job. He knows nothing of her family other than that she sends money home to them.

"I just got caught up in it all. I mean, you've been such a great guy, and I've really enjoyed getting to know you this last year."

Law wants to stop her, to say that they don't really know that much about each other. Maybe she's talked about a few of her dreams, but they don't speak of their family or pasts. Which is all right with him because his story, his childhood, was only filled with pain and degradation. That's why he's worked so hard to rid this city of those depraved beings who ruin so many other's lives.

KILLING ROSIE

"Hey," Law says, poking her in the arm. "I got a dance from the most beautiful woman in this lounge. Can't complain about that."

Sunny rolls her eyes but smiles. "Well, you're sweet for trying to make me feel better."

Law opens his mouth to argue, but she'll either deny it even more or get embarrassed, so he leaves it alone. "I guess I'd better go. What do I owe you?"

A twinge of guilt shoots through him—he totally cheapened the moment, but Sunny doesn't appear to take it that way.

"Nothing. On the house for all the trouble I caused."

"You were no trouble." Never.

She smiles appreciatively. "On the house. But I want one more thing." She creeps over to the open door, peeks out, and then returns.

Her arms slink around his waist, and she hauls him close, his gray eyes meeting hers. Her soft lips crush his. They are a perfect fit, him and Sunny, and he wishes their lives could be different. That he could have a woman like her by his side.

He wants to keep the kiss going, but she breaks away.

This is just her job, he reminds himself.

"Good luck with your move," she says. "And make sure you come see me the next time you're in Staden."

"I definitely will." He pats her ass, she smiles, and then he slips out the door. He has no plans to return, but those plans could change.

Maybe.

Chapter Two

Five days 'til Rosie dies

At the outer edges of her village, Bedra, Rosie stops to admire the Heiland's gorgeous garden, standing in the shade of their giant willow tree. She takes a deep breath, savoring the fragrant scent of the deep red lilies, and leans against the top rail of the fence. She lifts her aching foot and rests it on the bottom rail. It's been a long walk back to the family home in Bedra, but she didn't want to spend money on a carriage ride, and now the smell of the pink and white flowers lured her over.

"Rosie, good to see you. Are you done working for the week?" Mrs. Heiland wipes her sweaty forehead, peeking from behind her perfectly globe-shaped boxwood shrub, shears in her hand.

"Yes. I took a leave of absence, so I have a few weeks to enjoy at home and at Nana's," she replies. She looks forward to the break, even if she is taking care of her grandmother. "I can't pass by your garden without stopping to smell. It's heavenly."

The light breeze blows the willow wisps, tickling her shoulder, and she slides down a bit.

Mrs. Heiland snips off a bunch of lustrous orange tiger lilies from behind her and hands them to Rosie. "Please take these home to your mother. I know things have been tough dealing with your grandmother's illness. How is she anyway?"

Rosie's shoulders fall. Nana's health is up and down, and lately it's been down more than up. "Her body is on the mend, but she still refuses to move to be with us. It's so silly because between the five of us, we can take care of her, but she won't leave her home."

There's more to it than that, but it's not for ears outside of the family. Grandmother won't live with Mother because they don't get along very well, but all the blame falls on Mother and her witchy ways. That's why Rosie is taking a few weeks to help Nana. Nellie's in school and can't leave, and Stina and Linn would be more work to Nana than help.

"Thank you so much for the flowers and say hello to Mr. Heiland for me."

"Will do, dear. And keep us updated on your grandmother."

Rosie strolls down the side of the quiet dusty road, and the gravel crunches under her feet. She wrinkles her

KILLING ROSIE

nose at the rancid manure in the middle of the road. People should clean up after their horses.

Her two-story brown house looms in front of her, shadowing the bright sun, and she stares at the flaking paint and upstairs broken window with tape covering the crack. Mother should be taking better care of the house, and with the three girls still at home, it shouldn't be hard.

Rosie sighs, avoiding the hole in the bottom step and goes to the weathered door. Maybe she can talk Nellie into helping paint while she is back in town.

The steps to the house creak, reviving the anxiety inside Rosie, but she takes a deep breath of the lilies and steps inside. Laughter emanates from the parlor, and Rosie unlaces her boots, stores them and her bag on the threadbare rug, and creeps towards the noise.

"Rosie!" A big ball of energy slams into Rosie, hugging her tightly. She sputters, trying to spit out Nellie's blonde curls and keep the flowers from getting crushed, but Nellie doesn't let go. It's been three long months since she's seen her little sister, the only reason she ever returns home.

Finally, Nellie releases her hold, and Rosie steps back to see the changes in her sister. Three months is a long time at fourteen. "You have boobies," Rosie whispers.

Nellie blushes but grins. "I know. I think they might get bigger than yours." She can't hold back her proud smile, but the thought only worries Rosie. She's dealt with the extra attention of overly friendly men for years because of her own large chest.

"You're probably right, and remember that boys will tell you they love you, just so they can see them. Don't fall into that trap." Rosie has been there and done that and doesn't want her sister to make the same stupid mistakes.

Someone snorts from the other side of the room, but Rosie knows from whom it comes. Stina snorts more than an angry pig. Rosie slaps on her polite smile and turns to Stina, who sits at the table playing cards with Linn.

"Hello, sisters," Rosie says.

Neither returns the smile, their pale faces pinched tight.

"Now that Rosie is home, she can give you lessons on how to use those abnormally large breasts to get what you want from men." Linn narrows her eyes as if to challenge Rosie, but she won't take the bait.

Despite having beautiful blonde curls, china white skin, and deep blue eyes, Linn and Stina have always felt less than Rosie. She understands their feelings but hates that they blame her. Never once has Rosie hit on any of the twins' boyfriends, but when the boys try flirting with Rosie, the girls accuse her of inviting their attention.

They don't believe that men can be dogs.

Steps echo into the room. Rosie spins around to see her mother's grim face and offers the lilies. "Mrs. Heiland sent these home for you."

"I thought you would be home earlier. Put them in water." Mother motions to the kitchen.

"I got a late start. I'm sorry." Rosie crosses the parlor floor and enters the doorway into the kitchen to get a vase. The only hug she'll ever receive in this house is from her little sister. Mother seems to prefer doling out slaps than hugs, which is one of the reasons why Rosie moved away.

She takes a quick peek around the kitchen looking for a wine bottle sitting out but sees nothing. Mother doesn't seem like she's been drinking, but the woman has learned to hide it well, until her rage spills out.

After filling the vase with water, Rosie brings the flowers out to the side table in the parlor.

Mother harrumphs. "Well, now that the day is gone, you might as well spend the evening with your sister. She's been whining all afternoon, waiting for you. Tomorrow we'll get to my list."

"Yes, Mother." Rosie stands at attention, waiting for her mother to finish.

"I'm not sure why your grandmother chose this time to steal you away. We need you here too." She crosses her arms and glares at Rosie, waiting for an argument, but Rosie keeps her mouth shut. Nana has been in the hospital, and if her selfish mother can't see that Nana is the one who needs her now, there's no point in arguing.

Their relationship has always been strained, but Mother's animosity towards Nana has grown over the years.

"Maybe you can talk her into selling the house. It's much too big for her." Mother almost sounds angry about it, but Rosie can't fathom why.

Nellie jerks up in her seat. "If Nana sells the house, will she live with us?"

"No." Mother frowns. "She would go into one of those old folks home."

"Oh." Nellie slumps again.

"Mother, if we sell Nana's house, and then we sell ours, we can move to a bigger one," Stina says. "Maybe we can move to Staden. There's so many more men there."

"We could be well-off and go to parties all the time," Linn says with dreamy eyes.

KILLING ROSIE

"And can I get a horse?" Nellie perks up again.

"Of course," Mother says.

"But why would we buy a bigger house just because Nana sells hers? It's not our money." And Nana's house isn't worth all that much money. It's not very big. And it's a few miles outside of a small town.

"Because your grandmother doesn't need that money anymore." Mother's face twists with anger, and she stalks out of the room.

A rap comes from the door, and Nellie jumps to answer it. A few moments later, she returns with Ebba, Stina's best friend.

"Rosie. Great to see you." Ebba gives Rosie a warm smile. Since Rosie is only a year older than Stina and Linn, they had many friends in common, much to the twins' annoyance. "Great timing. Nils' is having a party tonight, and I know he and the others would love if you stop by."

Linn sighs, and Rosie ignores it. Seeing her old friends would be lovely and seeing Linn and Stina annoyed that she's at their party will be even lovelier.

"Yes, I'd like that. But probably not until later because Nellie and I have a few games of dominoes to play. Right, sis?" Rosie winks at her little sister, and she nods enthusiastically. Nellie will love the wooden domino set Rosie found for her. She bought a matching set to bring to Nana too.

"Great. We'll catch up there." Ebba turns back to the twins. "You guys ready to go?" They nod, gather their stuff, and leave the room. Now it's just Rosie and her favorite person.

She turns to Nellie and smiles. "So I want to hear about everything going on, and then I have a surprise for you."

Nellie eyes Rosie, her eyes sparkling. "How about you show me what you have first, and then we'll talk."

Rosie lets out a laugh and heads to her bag to get the present.

That evening, Rosie sits on the swinging bench on the front porch of Nils' house with the charming and handsome Otto. His long legs rock the swing, and Rosie tries not to stare at his big brown eyes and wavy blond hair. The party has been a whirlwind of catching up with old friends and flames, and just as she was about to leave, Rosie ran into Otto. Now his arm stretches across her shoulder, and she breathes in his musky scent.

KILLING ROSIE

"I've always had a thing for dark beauties." Otto runs his fingers through her hair and releases the strands, sending them down to her chest. "Blue eyes. A cute button nose."

And big breasts too. Rosie reads it in his face, but she's used to guys wanting her for her chest, and it doesn't mean she's a whore like her sisters think. That's one of the things she worries about with Nellie—that the twins will make her feel cheap and tawdry just because she has large boobs.

"So are you that dark everywhere?" Otto blows a puff of air on her ear, sending a shiver down her back. It would be so easy to let things happen, to become the girl her sisters accuse her of being. Rosie isn't innocent, and she's never claimed to be, but she can count the guys she's slept with on one hand.

Now kissing. That's another story. She's shared kisses with many, many men, but that's all they are, and that's all it'll be with Otto.

"Of course." Rosie gives him a smile, and the bench stops moving. Otto tugs her head to his and smothers her lips, but when his hand slides to her breasts, she stops it. His lips creep down her neck, and she melts into his arms, letting out a sigh. He tries again to feel her, and she places her palm on his chest.

"It won't happen, Otto." She forces his hand away and cups it in hers, keeping him from trying again.

He sighs, but smiles, taking her chin in his hand. "You taste mighty fine, Rosie."

That's all the encouragement she needs, and she kisses him once more, glad that his hands now rest on the back of her neck.

"Ot-to," a voice screeches from behind them at the open doorway, and they both freeze mid-kiss.

"What the hell are you doing with my sister?" Linn stomps onto the porch, her blonde hair flying, eyes blaring.

Oh no. Oh no, oh no, oh no. This can't be happening.

"Sister?" He stares at Rosie, eyes agape, but she can't move. "Sister?" He looks to Linn. "I… I… I thought you left?" Otto jumps off the bench, his gaze swinging back and forth between the two girls.

Linn thrusts him off to the side and stalks in front of Rosie.

"I didn't know. He didn't—" Rosie tries to explain.

"You whore." Linn slaps Rosie, and she touches her stinging cheek, seeing the crowd gathering behind Linn. "You can't keep your hands off any guy. You just have to have them all for yourself. You're the biggest damn tramp in town, and everybody knows it."

KILLING ROSIE

"I didn't know," Rosie pleads. She never would've kissed Otto if she'd known.

"How could you? How could you do..." Linn's voice tapers off as her friends drag her back, most shooting nasty glares at Rosie. Ebba watches Rosie, eyes blinking, and Rosie mouths one more time that she didn't know, but Ebba drops her head and backs away.

The buzzing pounds in Rosie's ears, and she slides off the bench. Otto is stuck like glue to the porch, with a look of horror on his face.

"You cad!" Rosie shoves him backwards. She wants to pound on his chest, yell at him for deceiving both her and her sister, but the tears threaten to fall, and she runs away.

The dark night swallows her as she rushes down the street, not knowing what to do or where to go. She slows to a trudge and forces herself to keep moving. Her foot dips into a hole on the side of the road, and she tumbles to the ground. Pebbles and dirt embed into her palms, and she lies still for a few moments, wishing she'd never gone to the party. Otto is the one at fault, but she will take all the blame.

Slowly, Rosie pushes herself up.

She can't go home, not yet, so she drifts to the one place that's always given her peace, and crosses through the opening in the wrought-iron fence surrounding the town's cemetery. A squirrel scrambles up a tree as she passes on her way to her father's grave.

The twins call her queer because she feels comfortable with the quiet tranquility, but the memories of her father keep her warm. And the cemetery holds loved ones who once filled others' lives with joy.

At least the dead people don't condemn her every decision and don't accuse her of ruining their lives.

She passes all the ghostly graves and kneels on the grass at her father's stone to trace the letters of his name. Mother has never been warm and loving, but after Father died, she became so much worse, fell into the bottle, and often took her anger out on Rosie.

Visiting her father brings no solace this time. She has to go home and face what's probably waiting for her. She knows darn well that Linn went running to their mother, and that she'll skew everything to make Rosie look bad. And it won't matter that Otto kissed her first, or that he never mentioned Linn or any girlfriend, because it's always Rosie's fault. Everything.

There's no use putting off the pain, so she lumbers back to her house.

The light slips out between the cracks of the curtain on the parlor window, and Rosie pauses at the front door. Her hand trembles, and she grips the handle

KILLING ROSIE

to slip inside. She removes her shoes and makes her way right to the parlor instead of going upstairs.

Rosie's mother sits on the settee next to a teary-eyed Linn, the half-full glass of red wine at her side. "It's about time you got home, young lady," Mother snaps.

"She was probably with Otto again," Stina says, glaring from across the room.

"I wasn't—"

Mother jumps to her feet and stomps over to Rosie, her footsteps echoing through the room. "How could you? Your sister loved that boy." Hot wine-breath smacks Rosie in the face, but she doesn't flinch. She refuses to back down when she is not wrong.

"One day," Mother continues her tirade, thrusting her index finger into Rosie's face. "Only one day you're home, and you're rude and disrespectful. And now this?"

"I didn't—"

Mother backhands Rosie across the cheek, and Rosie falls to her knees, holding her searing skin. Hot tears gather in her eyes.

"Don't you lie to me." Mother stomps her foot next to Rosie's knee and winds Rosie's long brown hair around her hand. "Otto told us the truth. How he tried to say no to you, but you threw all your womanly wiles at him. That you flashed your breasts at him for god's sake." Mother yanks Rosie's hair, sending shots of pain through Rosie's skull. "All your sisters want is to find nice young men to settle down with, and you constantly throw yourself at them. You are a whore and a bad influence, and I'm tired of having you hurt your sisters."

Mother jerks Rosie to her feet and forces her in front of Linn. "Apologize."

If she doesn't apologize, Mother will only hurt Rosie again. Her words, her hand, her wooden spoon. The physical pain lasts for moments, but the scars inside Rosie run much deeper.

"I'm sorry." Rosie keeps her eyes cast down, but she can still see the smirk on Linn's face.

"Like you mean it," Mother shouts, shaking Rosie's head. Her scalp feels on fire, and she wants to rub it away, but she must not move.

"I'm sorry for trying to steal your boyfriend." Rosie hates herself for having to lie, but she has no choice.

Linn harrumphs, and Mother releases Rosie's hair and shoves her to the floor.

"Get up to your room. And I want you gone first thing in the morning." She steps her slippered feet onto Rosie's dirty blue dress. "And remember this, if I hear one report back from your grandmother about the shenanigans you pull, you will have me to deal with."

Mother moves back, the deepened scowl set in her face.

"Yes, Mother." Rosie crawls to her feet and slinks towards the steps. She reaches for the banister.

"And I think you can arrange your own transportation to Lakare."

Rosie gasps and spins around. Mother can't be serious. She has no money to hire a ride, and there's only one other option. "But that'll take me three days to walk." Through the Storttrad Forest road.

Alone.

"I'm sure a tramp like you can trade something for a ride," Mother growls.

Stina snorts, and Rosie cringes inside. She would never sell her body like that, no matter what her mother or sisters think. Her head aches, but she refuses to let them see her pain. Not until she reaches the landing upstairs does she allow the tears to fall.

Instead of going to her room, she sets off for the washroom, not wanting Nellie to see her so upset. She splashes some cold water on her cheeks to cool down. This journey will take her three days when a carriage ride would take one full day. Where will she sleep? On the side of the road? Or find a home and ask if she can stay in their barn? She barely has enough money for food, much less two nights at an inn.

Rosie tiptoes into the bedroom, glad to see Nellie's still silhouette. The second bed will remain empty; both Stina and Linn will sleep with Mother tonight. Rosie quickly removes her filthy clothes and slips on the nightdress.

The covers and warmth of her young sister's body welcomes her, and Rosie lets out a deep breath.

"I believe you, Rosie," Nellie whispers into her ear. "We all know Otto is bad news. He did it once before, but she just forgave him and took him back. She just likes him because he wants to be a lawyer someday."

Nellie throws an arm around Rosie's waist, and her lips tremble. She bites back the tears once again. In a few more years her sisters will torment Nellie like they do Rosie.

"Thank you," she sniffs.

Her sister's words give her little reassurance though, and they don't change the fact that Rosie's cheek is still stinging from her mother's slap, or that her heart is damaged from her mother's vicious words. And since her mother has ordered her to go, Rosie will pack in the morning and leave immediately.

KILLING ROSIE

"Can I brush your hair?" Nellie says, not knowing what Mother had done. Rosie's roots still hurt, but the brushing and braiding will relax her.

Nellie retrieves the brush and sits cross-legged behind Rosie. It doesn't take long to get the tangles out, but Nellie continues to stroke her brush through Rosie's hair. The tension in Rosie's shoulders seeps out slightly. It should be Rosie taking care of her little sister, not the other way around.

"What will you do to get to Nana's? Do you have money?" Nellie asks, separating Rosie's hair into three sections.

Rosie sighs. The walk will waste so many precious days with her grandmother. "I'll just walk."

"It'll take you three days."

"I know, but what choice do I have? I can't exactly steal a horse now, can I?"

"No." Nellie lets out a dejected breath and stops the braiding process. "But it's not safe to walk that windy road through the forest. There's lots of animals and…"

And thieves, Rosie finishes her thought. She doesn't have much to steal, and she'll be okay. Nana needs Rosie. She won't be able to care for herself when she gets out of the hospital.

Only one good thing came out of her mother sending her away early. Now she can get to Nana's sooner and put all this big mess behind her. But it'll be a long journey with lots of time to think, and that Rosie doesn't look forward to.

"Don't worry. I'll be fine." She squeezes Nellie's shoulder, hoping that the words are true. "I'm more worried about you. And Mother."

"She has been okay. She's only got mad at me a few times. Mostly when she's muttering about Nana."

"Has she hurt you?"

"No." Nellie answers much too quickly. Rosie tugs on Nellie's hand and turns her head, causing the braid to fall from Nellie's grip. "Nothing bad. She just slaps me sometimes. But only when she's been drinking."

"But she drinks every day." The pain fills Rosie. She's unable to take care of her sister living so far away. Maybe perchance, Nellie could live in Staden with her. There's a good school not far from Rosie's apartment.

But her heart knows Mother won't allow it.

"I stay away from her. I follow all her rules and go to bed early. Don't worry about me." Nellie's voice is determined, much stronger than a fourteen-year-old should have to be.

"I still do," Rosie says.

"And I worry about you too." Nellie wraps her arms around Rosie's neck and hugs her.

Chapter Three

Four days 'til Rosie dies

Law leans against his wagon staring at the house he's called home for years. Those four small rooms inside are cramped, but the backyard drew him here years ago. Large oak trees provided shade and his much-loved privacy, not to mention the way it quieted the noise from the street. A fenced yard kept out roaming children, and he had a sizable garden for his vegetables.

He can't wait to reach Stilla and sit and enjoy the complete silence, watch the sun rise across the hills.

His wagon is empty, but soon it'll be filled with some of his possessions, although many he'll be leaving behind. He'll donate much to the children's home because he can't fit it all in; besides, he has few attachments to the things in his home.

"There you are," a voice huffs. "You're a hard man to find."

Law's shoulders tense at the man he doesn't want to see. If he wasn't leaving in a few days, the

KILLING ROSIE

resentment towards Filip might blow out of him. All Law's years, he's taken pains to make sure nobody knew where his home was, even having a fake residence in a building downtown in case someone followed him, but now Filip is about to tarnish his peaceful home with his filth.

Law turns to face the man he did a job for once, a mistake he wishes he could take back. Not because the target wasn't guilty—he was, but because Filip has not left him alone since.

The job for Filip went well, and Law ridded the city of an awful man, a man who set buildings on fire for insurance money but ended up killing several children in a nursery school—one being Filip's son. The judge decided the man was innocent despite overwhelming evidence against him, and Law easily found proof that the judge had been paid off.

"How'd you find me?" Law asks.

That case happened years ago though, but Filip seems to think they are buddies, sometimes begging him for money, or asking him to join in on some sketchy deals.

Law knows better than that to get involved with Filip and his financial dealings. He had been an honest man before his son died, but he and his wife split, and Filip descended into a darkness he couldn't control.

"You're a hard man to find. I've been checking around for you everywhere." The smell of alcohol seeps out of the grungy man, and he swipes his ever-running bulbous nose.

"I've been busy." This is exactly the reason Law doesn't keep a permanent office. He clenches his hands and folds his arms. "What do you want?"

"We need to talk. I have an excellent deal for you." Filip sticks his hands in his pockets and rocks back and forth on his feet.

"I'm not interested." Not now, not ever.

"No, we have to talk." He shakes his head quickly and glances towards the yard. Law swings his head around to find his neighbor, the old Mrs. Carlsson looking their way.

"Good evening, Mrs. Carlsson." Law tips his hat and gives her a smile. He'll miss the grandmotherly neighbor, listening to her talk of her grandkids, and her pumpkin spice pie.

"Good evening, Lawson." She claps her hands, and her puppy, a rambunctious boy, runs over. After living next door to her and her brood of Border Collies, he's decided they would be a welcome addition at his farm too. Steady, strong, and dependable.

Law turns back to Filip, about to tell him again he's not interested in whatever deal Filip has.

KILLING ROSIE

"No. It's not that type of deal. It's another deal. A job, I mean. Maybe we need to go into the house and talk about it." Filip peers over at the retreating Mrs. Carlsson.

Law has two choices. Argue with Filip, try to get it into his thick head that Law doesn't want the job. But that'll just leave Law with a headache. Or invite him in and listen to his story. Let Filip ramble a bit and say he'll think about it. Law will be gone within a few days, so that's probably his best option here.

"Okay, let's go inside." Law leads Filip through his front door and into his main living area. The sofa is worn and comfortable, and he'd love to bring it, but there's not enough room in the wagon. "Have a seat."

Instead, Filip takes his place by the window and peeks outside.

"So what do you need help with?" Law asks.

"This is big." Filip sticks his hands in his pockets again and paces along the wall. "Arvid Lundberg," he says and stares pointedly at Law.

"Who's Arvid Lundberg?" Maybe he should have just chanced the argument with Filip in the street.

"Union Bank," Filip says and waits for the acknowledgment from Law. Union Bank is one of the largest in town, but Law's never heard of the guy. "He's been stealing money from the bank. He lives in this mansion in the Gardens. He's ruined so many lives."

"And?" Law asks. A thief like Arvid Lundberg might be a despicable lout, but Law doesn't take care of people with big character deficiencies. He took care of monsters who didn't deserve to live. Vicious killers and men who violated women and children.

"And he's been stealing money for years. Leaving folks destitute. With nothing." Filip's words rush out, but he stares over Law's shoulder and babbles on about the man for a bit. Filip wasn't as excitable when Law worked with him last time. Law waits for Filip to meet his eyes, but he never does.

Law opens his mouth to ask if Filip has a loved one who was cheated by Arvid Lundberg but changes his mind.

The sooner he gets Filip out of here the better.

"I'll do it." This is just easier. Law isn't about to take any money from the guy anyway. They can make an appointment to *collect* it next week.

"Good. This man is awful. He shouldn't be allowed to live." Filip heads for the door.

They haven't talked about payment though.

"Filip."

The man about jumps, and Law studies him intently. His face reddens as he faces Law.

"We need to talk payment?" Law says.

"Oh, of course. How much?"

"A thousand valuta." The number is high, way higher than the previous job, but Law always leaves room for negotiating as clients always try to.

What is he doing? He isn't doing this job, so he should've thrown out a lower number.

Bad habits die hard.

Filip stares at his shoes. "A thousand, okay. We can meet Monday to discuss more details."

No negotiating—interesting. Last time Filip argued for twenty minutes about the price.

Law steps to the door and holds it open for Filip, who rushes through without a goodbye and hustles down the street.

Even though he isn't taking the job, Law shuts the door and follows Filip, staying back far enough and hiding behind trees so the man doesn't notice.

Their walk takes them to a park a few blocks away. Filip approaches a man on a bench and takes a seat as Law slips behind a tree. He's not quite close enough to hear, so he jumps from tree to tree to get closer. His back rubs against the scratchy bark as he strains to hear the conversation. He doesn't know the man, but he knows where the guy works. Filip is meeting with a sheriff's deputy.

"You're sure he'll do it?" the gruff voice of the deputy asks.

Law peeks out quickly from behind the tree.

"I said yes. We're meeting on Monday." Filip sets his ankle across his knee, and his foot bounces. "So all my charges will be dismissed after I meet with him?"

"That's the deal."

That snake. Law can't believe it. Filip is setting him up to get arrested. Law wants to leap out and pound Filip into the ground, but that will only serve to get him arrested sooner.

He peers out from behind the tree. The two men are still facing away, so Law hurries in the opposite direction.

Filip did something, and he's trying to weasel his way out of his charges by turning Law in.

This changes everything. The sheriff is after him for some reason but has to manufacture a charge against him, so they have no proof of his past deeds if that's the case. It sounds like they won't arrest him until Monday, but Law can't chance it.

He has to get out of Staden now. Under the cover of darkness, he'll pack everything and take off. He can't risk his future because of this snake.

And it's not like he has anything he needs to stick around a few more days for. He wanted to stop by and visit Sunny Daze one last time to see if she got his note he left her the other day about that job opportunity, but he doesn't want to risk it.

No, it's time to get out of Staden.

Chapter Four

Four days 'til Rosie dies

Yet another wagon passes Rosie too quickly, stirring up the dust and dirt. At least this one gave her a wide berth. She'll have to be more careful when she gets into Storttrad Forest as she might not be seen as easily.

Saying goodbye to Nellie was hard, but she puts her sweet smiling sister out of her head. Grandmother needs her help, so Rosie will go where she is needed.

Fields of dandelions cover the yard she is passing, and she takes in the beautiful sea of yellow knowing the homeowner probably does not appreciate them. The quiet solitude of her walk will give her much time to think, and she already has many plans for projects she'll help her grandmother during the month they have together.

Baking, and gardening, and anything else that needs be done around the home.

Even though clouds dot the sky, her body heats, and she can't wait until she reaches the town where

KILLING ROSIE

she'll find a room for the evening. She has enough to cover those nights at the inn, which is good because she doesn't want to camp out in the Storttrad Forest, but she won't have much money for food. She hates to admit that she took money from the twins' stash in their bedroom, but they'll probably never notice. They pay little attention to where their money goes.

She shifts her bag to her other shoulder, carrying only a few changes of clothes and food. It's not heavy, but she's sure it will feel like it by the time she reaches her destination.

Humming some of Nellie's favorite tunes helps pass the day along, and soon the afternoon sun is high above her, her feet in need of a rest. She has a ways to go to get to Uppehall and wants to arrive before night falls.

She shouldn't have stopped so long to eat and speak with that woman who was tending to the garden, but the honeysuckle on the trellis smelled so sweet. Rosie takes a deep breath to smell the small bouquet in her hand. Too bad it won't last until Grandmother's, but she'll find some more flowers before she reaches the hospital.

A horse neighs next to Rosie, and she looks up, surprised to see a wagon stopped.

"Good day, miss." The man has a bright red nose from too much sun, and the tips of his peeling ears stick out of his blond hair.

She gives him a wide smile. "Good afternoon."

"I noticed from far back that you were walking. Can I give you a ride?"

Finally. So many people have passed her by, no matter how many wishes she made for them to stop. This will get her to her destination so much faster.

"Yes, I'm traveling to Uppehall. Is that on your way?"

"Sure is." He pats the seat next to him and offers his hand for her bag. She tosses it to him and climbs into the wagon.

The lines of hard work and sun are carved deep into his face, and she figures he must be ten years or so older than her.

"Elias Wallin." He offers his hand, and Rosie introduces herself. "Is your family expecting you in Uppehall?"

"No. It's just one stop on the way." She eyes the line of trees ahead, Storttrad Forest, which they'll arrive at shortly. She welcomes the coolness of the trees and the shade and the smell of the pine trees. "I'm on my way to Lakare actually to see my grandmother. She's in the hospital."

KILLING ROSIE

Elias snaps the reins, and the horses begin their trot. "Is she okay?" he asks.

"She is on the mend. I'll bring her home. Do you live in Uppehall?"

"Just on the north side. We have a small farmstead. My wife and four children."

"Oh, how old?" One day Rosie wants to settle down and live a quiet life with her husband and children. She doesn't need a large farm but hopes she'll have a yard plenty big to plant everything she'd like to grow.

Elias chatters on about his children, the youngest at four being quite the stinker. Rosie can picture the little blonde children who probably look just like their father. They'd have his big blue eyes and full red lips. It isn't long before they enter the forest, the tall pine trees towering over them, shading them from the sun.

"Do you have children yet?" He peers over at her. The wheel of the wagon hits a small hole, jarring Rosie, and she clutches onto her seat.

"No, not yet. Someday. So what is Uppehall like? I've never had a chance to visit the town. All she remembers from passing through on her trips is that it's small.

"Too many people. Too large." He sighs. "But it's always been that way. And where are you from?"

Rosie tells him of Bedra, of the small community that he'd probably enjoy, and soon they're entering the forest, driving under a canopy of trees. The coolness envelopes her, a satisfying change.

Lakare lies at the other end of Storttrad Forest, a city even bigger than Staden, and she can't wait to get a glimpse of the large lake it borders. Maybe she'll have time for a swim before Nana gets out of the hospital.

Probably not, but she can dream.

Elias keeps up the conversation, including his job. When people are looking for new homes to live in, he's the one who shows them available houses.

Soon, an hour passes. She's not sure how much farther it is to Uppehall, but they have to be getting closer. She's about to ask Elias, but the wagon slows, and he turns off the main road onto another narrower path, a trail really.

"Um, isn't Uppehall that way?" She knows it is but isn't sure why he'd turn here.

"Don't you worry. I'll get you there." He smiles at her, and his gaze drops to her chest, raising her hackles.

"Actually, I think you can just stop and let me out. I'll walk from here."

"I don't think so." His voice darkens. What is he doing? Where is he taking her? She glances behind her but can no longer see the main road.

KILLING ROSIE

"Please stop." Her voice trembles.

"I said no," he growls, anger marring his once handsome features. He slaps the reins on the horses, and they speed up.

She has to get out of the wagon, but how? She can't jump and risk a broken leg.

"No, it's not that. I need to relieve myself. I've been holding it for a while."

"We're almost there." His lips are pursed as he stares down the path in front of them. She has no idea what lies at the end or if he'll hurt her, or violate her. She shouldn't have taken a ride from him.

"I can't wait. I'm about to pee." She glances at the seat. "I'm serious. I don't want to pee on my skirt." If he refuses to stop, she just might do that to make him think twice.

Elias slows the wagon but snaps at her. "Okay, but you're leaving your bag here."

She can't leave it. It's not the clothes she's worried about, but the money. She'll have no way to pay for a room or food if she doesn't have her coin purse. But maybe having a few minutes to think will help her.

He holds the bag on the seat while she crawls down and disappears between a few trees. She has no choice. She has to run. When she returns, she'll grab her bag and take off through the trees for the main road. He won't follow her or leave behind his horses and wagon… she hopes.

Rosie clenches her clammy hands as she trudges back to the wagon, his eyes tracking her every movement. This is her only chance—she has to do this.

She arrives at the wagon and pretends to climb to the seat but instead plucks off her bag and takes off running the other way, entering the trees.

"Get back here," Elias yells.

Run. Stay focused. Put space between us. Rosie scans the trees ahead as she pumps her arms, trying to avoid obstacles as the loud crashing noises and Elias' angry shouts follow her. She's smaller and takes advantage of slipping through those tighter spaces.

"You'll regret running," Elias screams.

The leaves and twigs below her feet snap, and she takes deep breaths, but she has to keep going… Around the trees, jumping over a fallen log.

Her shirt catches on the branch and rips, but she must not stop.

"I'll catch you, and you'll pay for making me chase you." His voice sounds the same, and she doesn't dare look back to see if he's gotten any closer.

Rosie ducks under a large branch, hoping it'll slow him. Maybe she should try to find a big stick to hit him with.

KILLING ROSIE

But that'll never work. He's too big and strong. Her only hope is to keep running.

Her chest is on fire, and he seems to be getting closer, and angrier. She'll never see her grandmother, never see Nellie. She should have never gotten into his wagon.

The sound of dogs barking carries through the forest. Maybe if there are dogs, there are people. Of course she's all mixed up now, and for all she knows, she could be running towards wherever he was bringing her. She has to take that chance though that it's someone who could save her.

The barking gets closer, and suddenly the two dogs are in front of her.

Not dogs. Wolves. Their thick coats are gray and black and white. One snaps at her, she skids to a stop, and the other circles behind her.

Elias blasts through the foliage behind her and stops, grasping his chest and breathing as heavily as her. His hate-filled eyes narrow on Rosie, and he stomps towards her.

The wolf growls, and he jumps back, his mouth dropping, and takes in the whole scene, the two wolves surrounding Rosie.

Branches and twigs crack, leaves crunch, and a boy of about sixteen pops out of the trees in front of them.

"Who are you? Why you on my land?" he growls, just as mean as Elias. A black shotgun is in his left hand, not pointed at them, but in a tight grip, ready to raise at any moment, and a hatchet is in the right. He drops the hatchet to the ground.

"I'm so-sorry," Elias says. "My wife had to tinkle in the trees and then wandered off. We'll be on our way." Elias captures Rosie's arm, and she winces as his nails dig into her skin.

"I'm not his wife." She doesn't know what this boy is like, but she can't return to the wagon with Elias.

"Of course she's my wife," he says to the boy. "She's mad at me and just wants to run off. We're almost home though."

The boy wipes his black hair from his forehead with his grimy hand, his scowl not wavering. His shirt and pants are torn, so badly they probably are unable to be mended anymore.

He doesn't say a word, just stands there studying them.

"I'm not his wife," she repeats.

"Rosie, this is ridiculous. Let's go." Elias grasps her arms and yanks her away. She stumbles, and he jerks her upright.

KILLING ROSIE

"Stop," the boys says, but Elias keeps going. "I said to stop," he roars, and Rosie sees the two dogs at his sides, their teeth bared. Elias slowly turns around.

The boy points the gun at both of them. They're about to die right here in this forest. This boy will shoot them, or the wolves will maul them to death. Nobody will know where she is or what happened to her, and her body will rot amongst the dead trees of the forest.

"You just go on and leave her here." He motions to Elias, who stays frozen, his gaze trained on the long black barrel pointed their way. "I said go." The boy's angry voice sends a shudder through Rosie's body.

"Fine." Elias shoves Rosie to her knees and stomps away. What will she do now? She just traded one monster for another. There's no way she can run from the two wolves or the gun.

She wipes the tears from her eyes as he kneels in front of her and offers his hand.

Nellie. She'll never see Nellie's smiling face or hear her giggles.

"You all right, ma'am?" a tentative voice says.

Rosie looks into the boy's big brown eyes and sees compassion that wasn't there before. The gun lays at his side on the ground, so she takes his rough-skinned hand and stands.

Maybe he isn't as vicious as she first thought.

"Thank you for rescuing me. I was telling the truth. He's not my husband. I just met him. He was giving me a ride to Uppehall, and then he turned off the road. I don't know where he was going."

"I know, ma'am. I got three sisters, and I ain't never seen one of them look as scared as you. And they fight a lot with their husbands."

"Well, thank you. I don't know where he was bringing me or what he was going to do." She doesn't want to think about it.

"Nothin' good. Alls that's down the drive to the east is an abandoned house. Been for sale for years."

Which is why Elias was bringing her there.

"Name's Viktor Byquist. These here are my lands. My parents' lands." His hands sweep out as if to showcase the forest. "I'm 'fraid I don't have a wagon to give you a ride, but I'll escort you to the outer edges of Uppehall."

Viktor leans over and snatches his gun, finds the hatchet, and gives a whistle. He trots away, the wolves following. Rosie has no idea how far in the forest she is—she can't see anything but trees, but Viktor's steps are confident as he strides away. She rushes after to catch up.

"How far away from town are we?" she asks.

KILLING ROSIE

"Bout a half hour." He glances back at her and smiles. "Depending on how fast you are."

She laughs. This boy with the dirty face and grimy body is her savior. Who knows what would've happened to her without him.

He says few words as they hike through the forest, and finally they reach the road.

"Thank you for getting me here. You don't have to go any farther. You've done so much."

"No, ma'am. My momma'd whip me bright red if she knew I let you go alone." He grins and continues hiking along the edge of the road. The wolves follow along but stay in the trees. "We're not much farther."

Pretty soon the town comes into view, and sure enough, he accompanies her to the very first buildings.

"I'm looking for an inn to stay at. Can you tell me what you recommend?"

He purses his lips and seems to be thinking hard. "I don't know the name, but it's the big blue one on the corner. There's only two on that street over there, so you'll find it." He points down one of the roads into town.

"Thank you again." She throws her arms around Viktor and hugs him. He saved her and went out of his way to help her. After she releases him, he steps back, a blush covering his face.

"Just doing my duty. Have a good day, ma'am." He gives her a wave and shoots off down the road. She watches him until he disappears into the trees. A flash of movement catches her eye. One of the wolves.

She isn't sure if they're really wolves, but their coloring, their size sure seems like it. She should've asked, but it's too late now.

Rosie hefts her bag onto her shoulder and heads down the street. Perhaps someone can direct her to the blue inn. A woman.

She wants to stay away from men for the time being, and when she leaves town, she'll find a stick to carry with her on her journey to protect herself.

There could be other monsters like Elias on this road, and one thing is sure. She won't accept a ride from a strange man again.

Chapter Five

Three days 'til Rosie dies

Law takes a long sip of deep red cranberry juice and reviews the notes for his job while the chattering of diner patrons continues all around him. Very soon he can set down roots in a new home. Stilla is so close he can almost taste the fresh, clean air and the quiet nights without the hustle and bustle of the city. Killing Rosie will be the last step, and then he's free.

Most jobs have a tricky part, witnesses to work around, but this one will be easy. If the house Rosie will be staying at is as secluded as the sisters said, he'll have no problems with nosey neighbors. A simple job.

Luckily he tied up his last few loose ends before Filip found him, and he was able to leave right away. Just had one stop to visit an old friend to say goodbye, but now, after his last bites of food, he's on his way. He waves to the pretty barmaid for his bill.

No way.

Law squints, trying to get a closer look at the woman sitting at a table. He'd recognize those deep blue eyes and the beautiful dimpled cheek anywhere. And those breasts. Dark brown hair cascades down her shoulders, which means that her auburn locks at the lounge are a wig. Not a surprise.

He watches Sunny for a bit. Any time someone speaks to her, she smiles, but as soon as they leave, the smile fades away, replaced by a sadness that makes his heart ache.

He should just walk away, but she looks so lonely. He has to go say hello.

No, he *wants* to say hello. The memory of her lips on his invades his mind. He definitely needs to say hello. Law runs a hand through his hair and makes sure he has no food on his face, and then he wipes his sweaty palms on his trousers, feeling like an idiot for being intimidated by this woman. She's just a dancer from a lounge.

But she's not, and saying she's *just* a dancer is demeaning. He knows she's so much more.

Law sneaks around behind her and whispers in her ear. "Hey, doll, you're not following me, are you?"

Her eyes fly open, and the bleakness disappears. "Law, what are you doing here?" She scans the diner as if searching for something. Maybe she's with someone, a jealous boyfriend. Even though she didn't get into her personal life too often, he figured she had no husband. No decent man would allow his wife to work in such a place. Law would work twenty hours a day to keep his wife away from such a place.

"Just having a bite to eat on my way out of town. Remember, I told you I was moving?"

"Oh, I..." She digs in her bag, glancing around. "Why don't we go outside and talk where it's quiet. I'll meet you out front in a few minutes." She smiles, and he takes his hint and heads outside.

He waits by his wagon, petting his horses. Sunny exits the restaurant, her long blue skirt flowing behind her as the sun's rays light her gorgeous head. She's beautiful with her dark locks. Hell, she'd be stunning with no hair.

She bounces over and reaches out to hug Law, and all the activity around him ceases to exist as he wraps his arms around this radiant flower-scented woman.

"It's so good to see you. And what a coincidence. I'm on my way out of town too." She shields her eyes from the sun and steps towards the horses. "What stunning creatures." Her hand runs down the horse's neck, making Law wish he was the horse right now.

"Yes, they've been hard workers. So where are you headed?"

She frowns. "Um, Lakare. I'm visiting my grandmother."

"A vacation, huh. You deserve it." He chuckles, unable to keep his eyes off her. What he wouldn't give to have a pretty lady like her to take care of him. Bathe him. Feed him. Love him.

Love. Law almost snorts, shaking off the ridiculous feeling.

"Yes, a short one." Her lips form a tight line.

"Can I give you a ride to your coach? I assume you're leaving soon." He points to the bag she set on the gravel.

"No thank you. I'm walking,"

He scoffs. "You can't walk to Lakare." That'll take her several days. Not to mention being a woman alone on the heavily forested road with a lot of sketchy men. "I don't think so. Hop in. It's on the way to Stilla." And also Radda, which is where he'll be stopping for Rosie.

She stares at the ground, biting her lip. "You don't have to do that. I enjoy the solitude."

Her expression doesn't match her words.

"Sunny," Law says, resting his hand on her shoulder, "If you think I'll let you walk to Lakare, you're crazy."

She offers a grateful smile and takes his hand to climb into the wagon, and Law admires her sweet ass.

KILLING ROSIE

He hitches up the horses and climbs into his seat. Sunny remains quiet on the ride out of town, the only sound the clomping of the horses. It's like the gabby girl has disappeared.

"Do you visit your grandmother much?" he asks.

Her face lights up.

"Not a lot since I moved to Staden. It's hard to get time away with all my jobs."

"Did you ever check into that job at the nursery?"

"Yes, thank you so much for the recommendation. But it was filled already."

"Oh." Law slumps in his seat. He'd stopped to visit a friend the day after he saw Sunny last and found out they had an opening. Sunny wasn't at the lounge when he went to tell her, but he left her a note.

"It would have been a wonderful position. I would've been able to work with plants, and I'm sure I would've learned so much."

That job would've been perfect for Sunny. Decent paying, but more importantly, it would've been something she loved. Plants and flowers. She seems to know everything about them.

I love digging in the soil, she said once, *helping the plants to thrive. Seeing the beauty, even in the simplest of plants. Someday I'll attend the university, and then I'm opening my own nursery or flower store. I'm not sure what yet.*

"There'll be other opportunities," she says, staring off into the trees.

"Perhaps I should hire you to be a farmhand. You can dig in the dirt all you want." He chuckles.

"Well, now, if you farmed closer to Bedra, I would take you up on that, but Stilla is quite a journey away, isn't it?"

"About a week." An isolated farm miles away from a small village is just what he wants.

"I'm pretty sure I'd miss my family. Besides, I have several opportunities in Staden. I just need to earn some money now and save it for Nellie. She'll soon be a woman, and I know my mother won't have any money for her to go to the university when she graduates. She's so bright, and I want her to have a future."

"So you've skipped the university so she can go?" The more he finds out about Sunny, the more he likes her.

"My mother and other sisters won't help her, and that's why I started at the lounge. Dancing in front of randy men isn't really my favorite thing to do, but once I send money to my grandmother and mother, I still have leftovers for Nellie's school fund."

Life would've been different for Law if he had a big sister like Sunny. Selfless and generous. The kind of woman he'd like to spend his life with, working the land, fishing and hunting, and taking care of her.

He pushes the thought out of his mind. A woman like Sunny deserves better than a killer like him, but the irony isn't lost, that he's sitting in a wagon with a woman whose life mirrors his. He learned to survive at an early age and somehow fell into a life he never wanted or expected.

Killing people isn't fun. He doesn't get any enjoyment out of it because his jobs are all revenge killings for someone else. Payback for those people who wreaked havoc on others' lives with their torture or abuse.

"Your sisters won't help either? Or your mother?" Doesn't sound like she comes from a loving family.

"My sisters are lazy, and my mother drinks too much." She releases a deep sigh. "Red wine. Always too much red wine."

Law understands that. "Tell me about Nellie," Law says, and Sunny gives him the biggest smile yet.

An hour down the forested road, Sunny yawns. She hardly took a breath telling him all about her little sister and how fun and sweet she is, along with several silly stories.

Nellie sounds like a copy of Sunny, and he tells her so.

Sunny giggles. "She's better than me. She'd never work as a dancer." The gloominess seeps back into her voice, and Law wants to wipe it away.

"She'd be lucky to turn out like you. Hardworking, willing to do anything for a family member."

Her smile warms Law inside, and he lets out a laugh when it turns into another yawn.

"I'm sorry." She slaps her hand over her mouth. "Didn't mean to show you my tonsils."

Law keeps his face serious. "They are the most beautiful tonsils I've ever seen."

Sunny bursts out laughing, and he pats his shoulder. "If you want to rest your head, I've got this soft, plush shoulder here."

"Actually," she says with a mischievous grin, "I see something much better." She runs her hands over his thigh, sending sparks through his body.

"You can't hold me responsible if you hit something hard."

"I'll take my chances." She grins again, getting hit by another yawn.

She lays her head on his lap, and he brushes her hair behind her ear. Despite all the bumps from the gravel road, she falls asleep within minutes. Now Law has a terrific view of her cleavage, which he gratefully admires.

KILLING ROSIE

An hour into her nap, Law makes a stop to get the horses a drink, and Sunny stretches. Her dress had crept up her lean legs during the ride, and Law is disappointed to see them recovered.

"Water?" He offers her his canteen, and she throws back her head and takes several sips of the cold water. Law ignores the urge to run his fingers down her smooth neck to that sexy dip at her collarbone.

"Thank you, kind sir." Sunny hands the canteen back, the brightest, most beautiful smile on her face. "Now I must step away to the ladies' room." She climbs out of the wagon, and he follows the swish of her dress as she heads into the general store.

After attending to the horses, he wanders up the creaky wood steps. Sunny leans against the front counter on her elbows, her hands waving as she speaks with a dowdy old woman. The blue skirt with yellow flowers accents Sunny's curves, yet appropriately covers all those parts women don't like to show.

"Good day." A weathered man behind the counter nods, and Law tips his hat and repeats the greeting back. The old man's eyes flick to Sunny and linger a few seconds too long.

Law shoves away the jealous pang; he has no right to hold such feelings.

"Oh, Law, look over here. Mrs. Toten has the most delicious pastries, and I can't decide." Sunny waves him over and slings her arm through his to pull him closer to the counter. "My grandmother works magic in her oven. I'll be helping her recuperate from her hospital stay, and I'm sure she won't be doing any baking, so maybe I'll try your red raspberry tart, please."

"Yes, ma'am. Anything for you, sir?"

"No, I'm fine, thank you." Hospital stay? Sunny has only mentioned visiting her grandmother. He hopes it's nothing serious.

"I'd better go relieve myself now," Sunny says. "I sort of forgot when I walked in here and smelled the fresh baked bread. Please excuse me."

Law watches Sunny glide to the back of the store and out the door before wandering around the store to stock up on a few supplies. As he pays the bill, Sunny zips back inside.

"My mouth is watering, thinking about that tart." She smiles at the woman. "How much do I owe you?"

"The gentleman paid already." The woman pushes the sweet treat across the counter.

"Thank you, Law. That was very sweet of you. I suppose I must share a bite with you then." She laughs softly and takes a bite. "Delicious." She nods at the woman.

KILLING ROSIE

Sunny gushes about the pastry before switching over to the topic of gardens, and the beautiful flowers the woman has behind the store. Law stands next to Sunny, listening to her and the woman talk like old friends.

Time passes quickly, and Law figures the horses must be done eating. "Excuse me, ladies. I need to prepare the horses."

"Oh yes, we'd better get going. I've wasted too much of your time." Sunny's cute face wrinkles up in concern.

"I'm in no rush," he assures her and heads out the door.

The two girls look ready to go. Beautiful brown mares, sleek, but strong. Law runs his hand down Minnie's head. "Just a bit longer, girl, then we'll make a stop."

They could probably make it to Lakare tonight without pushing the girls too hard, but Law doesn't want to drop Sunny off that late at night. Of course spending the night with her at some cozy inn along the way would be a big plus.

Law gives Misty a scratch behind her ears, and she lowers her head for him.

"They're magnificent," Sunny says, and Law turns around to see her leaning against the railing on the stairway. "What are they like? Do they have different personalities? I don't know much about horses." Sunny shrugs and saunters down the steps.

"Definitely. Minnie is dependable, inquisitive, and friendly. Misty is friendly too, but she's got a stubborn streak in her. She makes life more fun."

"I've never ridden a horse. I'd like to try sometime."

"Then you can ride Minnie when we stop for the day. She'll be perfect for you."

"I'd like that, thank you." Sunny lays her soft hand on Law's arm, sending his nerves on edge. That smile is amazing. Sunny stares at him, her hand sliding up and down his arm. "I have a lot to thank you for, and maybe later I'll get that opportunity."

She winks and hops into the wagon before he has a chance to help. She swishes her dress under her ass and sits. All he can think about is kissing those beautiful lips, making love to her, and holding her in his arms.

"You'll catch some flies with that open mouth." Sunny giggles, and Law snaps his mouth shut. Ridiculous. He doesn't get excited about women. Not in that way at least.

He crosses around the wagon and jumps in. Sunny is quiet as they pull away.

KILLING ROSIE

"The tart was nowhere near as delicious as Nana's," she whispers, peering back over her shoulder.

"Don't worry," Law whispers back. "I don't think she can hear you."

She punches him in the arm. "Law!"

He likes the way his name rolls off her tongue.

"Nana's showed me how to make her tarts, but I never paid attention. I will this time. She'll probably spend a lot of time resting in bed, and I'll need something to do."

"Is she sick?"

"Yes, she's in the hospital, but she'll be out soon."

"Your grandmother is lucky to have you help her."

Sunny lets out a slow breath, her smile dropping from her face. "I didn't have much of a choice. I mean, I want to help her. I love her dearly, and I'd do anything for her, but…" She runs her hand back and forth over the rough wood seat, and Law worries she might get a sliver in her delicate skin.

The silence lingers, the only sound the clip-clopping of the horses' hooves on the gravel.

"My sisters refused to go. Well, the older two. They have no jobs and do nothing all day, and Nellie needs to stay in school. And Mother… She blames Nana for all the ills in her life. Mother can be nasty, and when she's angry, she'll get right in Grandmother's face and shake her fist. I've even seen her shove Nana around a little, but at least I've never seen her hit her. She must have a slight modicum of respect at least for her mother. Not like her children—we're fair game."

That bitch. Law is often a witness to the evil inside others, but he's never understood how a parent can hurt their own child. His mother never beat him, but she sent him off for others to do so. Desperation can do horrible things to a person, but it's the ones who enjoy inflicting pain who are the worst.

Law sets the reins on his lap and searches her face. "She hits you?"

"Oh no. I didn't mean it like that. She has a wicked slap, but she doesn't beat us or anything." Sunny stares ahead, absentmindedly touching her cheek.

Law snorts. It probably happens a lot more than Sunny wants to admit.

"My mother's had a hard life," Sunny says. "She's done everything for us since my father died. I know she loves us, but she doesn't always show it."

Sunny sounds as if she's trying to convince herself more than him. Even though he's lived a life of violence, he'd never inflict such harm on an innocent life. And children are innocent. He had been innocent at one time, and that innocence was brutally stripped away.

KILLING ROSIE

Law studies her face for a moment. "My father died from the bottle, and my mother sold me off to pay his debts." At ten years old, Law was forced into a life no child deserved. Too little sleep, too little food, and too much back-breaking work.

Sunny's face falls. "How could a mother do such a thing?"

Law brings his gaze to meet Sunny's, to see the sorrow consuming her face. "She didn't have much of a choice. The man who held my father's debts was not a good man."

He still can't clear his mind of the night Donaldson came to collect the money from his mother. She couldn't pay him off, so he took her body, and Law spent the night listening to her cries as Donaldson violated her.

For two weeks, strange men entered their home at all times of the day. Mother would disappear into the bedroom for a short time, and once the man left, she remained in her room for the next hour crying. And then Donaldson came for Law and sold him to the factory owner who worked him like a slave at age ten.

Six years later Law heard his mother died. He chose to take control of his life, and he sought out Donaldson. It was the only time Law took somebody's life out of personal revenge.

Maybe this is why he feels such a desire to finish off Rosie. He doesn't want to admit that one part of him considered making her death rougher than he should, make it painful.

Over the years, he developed his style. Law always explained to the target why he was dying. He enjoyed hearing them beg for forgiveness for all the atrocities they'd committed, but he didn't prolong their death. He delivered justice swiftly, and even though he despises the things Rosie is doing, he won't deviate from his plan.

"Are you okay?" Sunny says, snapping Law out of his trance. His face burns hot at the thoughts screaming through his head. Law shouldn't be thinking about Donaldson and the horrors he caused with this beauty beside him.

"Yes." He pushes away the hatred in his body. "For a few years I worked on a farm. Me and the other kids worked fifteen-hour days in the field, but surprisingly, it stoked my love of the earth."

"Will you have animals on your farm?"

He silently thanks her for changing the subject. He doesn't want to think about this job or Rosie. She's no different from Donaldson, is doing the same thing, but maybe it's worse. Rosie is subjecting her little sister to such heinous acts, a girl she supposedly loves. It's worse than what Donaldson did to a woman he cared nothing for.

"Eventually yes. Cattle, but I hope to have some chickens and pigs on hand, mostly just for myself. But I'll probably grow barley or oats. They're well suited to the soils."

"And flowers. You must have a flower garden too. Twinflowers, mums, roses." Sunny closes her eyes and takes a deep breath.

"And definitely some gerbera daisies," Law adds.

"Oh my, yes. I love daisies." She smiles, then turns to Law. "You know about flowers too? Is there anything you don't know about?"

"Not much," he says with a wink, and Sunny laughs.

Law lucked out, running into her. A beautiful woman by his side, someone to talk to on a long trip, but best of all, he knows the fun they'll have later when they finish what she started at the lounge.

"Room number five." The man at the small inn hands Law a key attached to a red plastic tag. "Have a good stay, Mr. and Mrs. Wolf."

Sunny giggles, and the man gives them a look. She throws him a quick thank you.

Law follows her up to the third floor, her curvaceous body calling out to him with every step. All he's thought about for the last half hour is touching her perfect skin, making love to her beautiful body.

Down boy.

Sunny flips her head around, her hair flying. "Are you checking out my backside?"

"Can you blame me?" He shrugs, keeping his voice cool, and she laughs again.

At the top of the steps, she spins around. "Now I want you to know that I'm sleeping with you because you're sexy as hell, and not just because you've treated me so well."

Law grasps the back of her neck to bring her inches away from his lips. His other hand runs down her back to finally squeeze that plump ass.

"The reason doesn't matter to me."

His mouth blazes into her luscious lips, a mix of flowers and wine from their earlier meal, and she lets him take the lead. Her kiss is intoxicating and brings him to places he hasn't been for a while.

He slams her back into the wall and kisses her neck.

"Where's"—she pants, trying to catch her breath—"Where's the room?"

Law raises his head and realizes they're still in the hallway. He straightens out her shirt and takes her hand to kiss it. "This way, doll."

Inside, Law watches Sunny float around the room in her flowing skirt. She pauses at the window to gaze outside, and he steps behind her and lifts her long hair to run his fingers through the thick, soft strands. He twists her hair and lays it over her neck, exposing her smooth white skin.

Her neck tastes salty and sweet as he nibbles to her shoulder. His whole body burns for hers, but he slowly unbuttons her shirt, and it slips to the floor. The skirt soon follows.

She slides one of his buttons through the hole, then leans in to his lips, but only a quick kiss, leaving him thirsting for more.

Another button, another kiss. Then one more. Damn. How many buttons does he have on this stupid shirt?

Both their clothes are soon lying on the floor, and they enjoy each other's touch, exploring each other's bodies, and finally making love.

Law collapses onto her, their sweaty bodies meshing together.

"That was…" Sunny blinks her bright eyes.

Fantastic… Perfect.

"Yeah, I know." He slides off and rolls on his side.

"You sure you want to retire to Stilla?" Sunny sighs.

Law runs his finger between her creamy white breasts. His skin seems so dark next to hers.

"I'm having second thoughts." And thirds. And fourths. He'd love to sweep away his past, pretend it didn't happen, but this one night of unbelievable sex with this incredible woman doesn't change anything. After this last job, he won't be a killer anymore, but he'll be a former killer, and that's no better.

"And I'm thinking of running away to Stilla with you." She closes her eyes, a dreamy look on her face.

"And will you pack your little sister and grandmother along with you?"

"I know." The sigh that follows her words drains Law. This is how it must be, no matter what his feelings.

"Sunny, doll, how about we forget about all that for now?"

She stares at him, intense. "Law, I think I should—"

"Let's just enjoy the night and each other. Because I've got many other things I'd like to do to your body."

KILLING ROSIE

He lowers his lips to her belly. They only have one night together, and he wants to make the most of it.

Chapter Six

Two days 'til Rosie dies

Rosie stares at the man in the bed next to her, the dark stubble on his square chin, the closed lids covering his steely gray eyes. She'd wanted one night of distraction from all her worries, and he provided what she needed. His kisses were passionate, his touch set her on fire, and when they were done, he let her fall asleep in his strong arms.

She closes her eyes and breathes in deeply. No more silly boys like Otto; she needs a man. Rosie almost laughs. A man. When will she ever have time for a relationship? After Grandmother gets back on her feet, Rosie will return to Staden to work her two to three jobs. It's all for Nellie's sake, to eventually get her out of the house and away from her mother and sisters.

Rosie's gaze slides down from Law's face to his toned chest. He was so sweet for finding her that job opportunity that other day. How she wishes she could've worked at the nursery, although this visit with Nana may have kept her from getting the job anyway.

First a job, then a ride to Lakare, saving her from traveling the worrisome road alone and running into men like Elias, and now a room at a cushy and extravagant inn with its vase of red silk peonies on the dresser, carpeted floors, and luxurious linens. And the walls. She can't get over how last night she heard not one door slam nor a noise from their next-door neighbors.

Law's eyes open, and a grin spreads across his lips. "Good morning, doll." He runs a hand through his short black hair and lays his head on the pillow again.

"Good morning." She loves when he calls her doll, but he probably calls all the women that. He's such a gentleman—Nana would love him.

"You look like you have much on your mind."

She can't exactly tell him that she thinks her grandmother would love him, so she shares the other thing floating through her head.

"I'm just grateful I ran into you. I'm spending enough time worrying about my grandmother, and I didn't think about how dangerous this journey might be. You saved me from any more trouble."

"More trouble?" Law's face clouds over. "Did something happen?"

"I accepted a ride from this man, and he…" Her memories of running through the forest flash through her mind. Elias' yelling and threats, the way he grasped her arm. "Well, he did nothing to me because I had a bad feeling and ran from his wagon."

Law clenches his jaw, his eyes darkening.

"He chased me through the forest, but I ran into this boy who rescued me." Viktor and his wolves. "He escorted me to town."

"Did he hurt you?" Law grips her arm and examines her body intensely, as if he might've missed some bumps and bruises.

"No. I was okay. I came to the inn that night and then ran into you in the morning." She motions to the rest of the room. "And now we are here."

"What's his name? I think I need to go back and *talk* to him," Law growls. She has no doubt he'd do more than talking. But although having Law beat Elias to a bloody pulp would give Rosie some satisfaction, she knows it's wrong. Law cannot be the judge and jury.

"He didn't actually do anything to me. If he'd done something, I could go to the sheriff, but he didn't really have a chance." Almost though. It had been close. But she had little to tell the sheriff, only that Elias had chased her through the woods and threatened her.

KILLING ROSIE

"Even so, I think it'd be good to pay him a visit," he says with all seriousness.

And he would. "No, I mean I don't know his name." It's one little lie, and another won't hurt. "And I don't think he was from around there anyway."

"Sunny." He shakes his head, a grimace on his face.

"I know. I was a bit foolish, but I didn't have the money for a carriage ride."

"You are a brave woman." He pulls her forward and kisses the top of her head, then falls back into the pillows. "I'm sure you want to get on your way to see your grandmother."

Rosie stretches and climbs out of bed. She slides the curtain open, and a moth flies out and lands on the sill.

"I'll get that." Law jumps out of bed and grabs his boot.

"I'll just open the window." Rosie unclicks the latch and tugs the window up. With a quick wave of her hand, the moth flies outside. She shuts the window, then turns and leans against the wall. Her tummy rumbles, loud.

"Hungry? We can get breakfast." Law grins, dropping his boot to the floor, and lies in bed again, his gaze washing over Rosie.

This inn even serves a free breakfast to its patrons, so different from the one she cleans rooms at.

"I guess so." She pats her tummy and returns to the bed to sit, sinking down next to Law and his bare chest with its rippling muscles.

Last night had been tremendous, but now she's suddenly feeling shy in her thin nightdress. It's such a silly feeling considering how she dances in front of all those men, but this isn't a stage at the lounge, and she's not performing for some random man whose name she doesn't know.

Law reaches over and slides his hand up her leg. His rough skin is that of a man who works with his hands.

"I'm hungry for you, Sunny-girl." His grin sends a rush of flutters through her body, and for a moment she feels stupid. She should tell him her real name, but what does it matter? They'll never see each other after today.

His sudden kiss, the feel of him pressing into her, heats her body. She allows herself to drown in the pleasure he offers… one last time.

KILLING ROSIE

Rosie stands on the wooden sidewalk, the hospital in Lakare looming behind her, a bouquet of colorful sweet pea in her hand. Wagons and carriages fill the roads, just like in Staden. She waves at the man who has been so generous as he drives away on the long start of a journey to the north.

It's a shame he'll be so far away. Despite being a man who frequents her lounge, he's an upright guy, sweet and fun, and if she met him in a different life, she wouldn't mind spending more time with him.

But now she needs to see her grandmother.

She waits until he's so far down the road that she can't tell which wagon is his anymore and steps through the tall wood hospital doors. Several people stand at the desk to find out room numbers of their loved ones, and Rosie waits her turn, watching the visitors pass by and the nurses rushing through the halls. This hospital is bright and cheery like the one in Staden, and she's glad Nana came here instead of depending on the doctor in Radda.

Rosie's mother should be here—this is her mother—but she doesn't care. The disappointment over her mother's actions is strong, but she is not surprised. Mother often complains of Nana, of how disrespectful and stingy and harsh she is, but Rosie has never seen that side of Nana. It's like they look at the same woman and see two completely different people.

But Mother looks at Rosie the same way, believes she is lazy when she works several jobs. Mother never says thank you for the contributions Rosie makes to the family.

After getting the room number, Rosie marches up the steps to the fourth floor and quietly opens the door to the room. The woman in bed looks nothing like the grandmother she saw last: paper-thin skin, sunken eyes, and a gaunt frame. Rosie can barely focus on the fragile body sleeping in the hospital bed. Tears fog her eyes. Mother never said Nana was doing so badly. If she had, Rosie would have visited much sooner.

"Nana?" Rosie says tentatively, grasping onto her boney hand. A tube sticks out of her arm, hooked to a bag next to the bed.

The old woman opens her dull eyes. "Rosie dear. You're here." Her scrawny fingers give Rosie's a squeeze.

"Look what I brought for you." She holds up the sweet pea bouquet, and Nana's eyes widen, a smile stretching across her lips.

"Can I smell them?"

Rosie holds the flowers still in front of her grandmother's nose, and Nana takes a deep breath and quickly falls into a coughing fit, shaking her body. She sounds phlegmy like she has liquid in her lungs.

Rosie sets the flowers on the shelf.

"Are you okay? I thought we were going home." She is supposed to be taking Nana home to mend, but Nana can't leave the hospital looking like this. The hospital should have contacted them, but maybe she's not as bad as she looks.

Nana grimaces, and Rosie slides the stringy gray hair off her face. She coughs once again, and Rosie struggles not to let the tears fill her eyes.

"Don't cry. It's my time, and I'm okay with that. I've missed Pappy so much, and I know he's patiently waiting for me." Another violent cough wracks her body, and Rosie scoots in closer.

"Don't talk like that, Nana. I'll call the doctor in. You'll be fine." She doesn't quite believe those words, but she can't give up hope.

"No, I've told the doctors I want no more medicine. I've been waiting for you to come, and now I'll ask them to remove the bag." She glances to the tube in her arm.

Rosie bites her trembling lip, unsure if there is even enough time to let her mother know, to call on Nellie to say goodbye. Maybe Nana is just talking nonsense; maybe she needs sleep.

"Just rest, Nana. I'm here now. You get some sleep, and then we'll talk."

"Sing me a song," Nana says. "I've always loved the sound of your voice. Just like your Pappy."

Rosie's throat tightens up, and she takes a moment to gather her strength. Nana needs her now, and she has to make her comfortable. Maybe when Nana falls asleep, Rosie can find a doctor and find out how they can help her.

She opens her mouth to sing a tune Nana taught her years ago, and a withered hand, black and blue with transparent skin, grasps Rosie's arm. "You know I love you."

"I know, Nana. I love you too." She chokes out the words. Life is hard to imagine without Nana. Sitting on the porch listening to stories, knitting projects they shared, working in the garden and baking in the kitchen.

So many things have happened lately, but none of those are important now.

Just Nana.

Rosie lays her head next to her grandmother, listens to the old woman's heavy breaths, and starts the song she knows Nana will love.

Chapter Seven

Two days 'til Rosie dies

She's just a woman.

Law repeats those words as he approaches Radda in his wagon. But one helluva woman. He has to get Sunny out of his mind though because he's got serious things to think about.

Rosie needs to die.

He digs out the rough map Stina and Linn made for him and adjusts his hat to shade his eyes. The map shows the route to the house, the future brothel she'll be at. They figured she'd be there any time, so after he scopes out the house and surrounding area, he'll continue on to the next town to find a room. Hopefully she hasn't already shown up. He can work around it, but he much prefers when things go to plan.

Radda seems to be a funny place for a brothel, the town so small, but there are probably enough men around and traveling through the area. Once word gets out, she'll have no lack of customers.

The turn off the main road arrives, and he sets off down the long drive through the thick green trees. No more houses around here, he was told, but he still keeps his eyes out. If someone is at the home when he arrives, he'll just say he is lost, and then he'll drop off the wagon and return at night under the cover of darkness.

The cottage lays in a small clearing, no movement in sight, so he parks the horses and saunters up to the home, taking in the two birch trees, one off each corner of the house. A weird spot to place two trees.

Nobody responds to his knock, and the door is unlocked, so he steps inside calling for Frank. Nobody answers, and he shuts the door so he can roam around the house freely.

The air is stuffy, and dust lines the shelves, but the home looks like it's been lived in recently. He checks out the two-bedroom home, studying the layout, and looks for all the objects the sisters told him would be here. Everything is exactly as they described, from the blue kitchen cabinets to the faded brown sofa covered with too many quilts, to the red check curtains on the windows.

This is the home where Rosie will be living with the little sister, the home she's turning into a brothel. It looks too comfortable, too normal, for what Rosie has planned, but maybe she'll make some changes. It's away from prying eyes, and that's what counts in this type of business.

He almost laughs at the cross-stitched picture on the wall that says *Bless This Home.*

He stares at the worn red and white quilt on the bed. Someone did a lot of work on it, and now Rosie's sister may be using this bed for horrific acts. Acts his mother was forced to perform by Donaldson.

Law's stomach sours. Donaldson made her a whore, forced her to be with vile men. His mother didn't deserve that, and neither does Rosie's sister. She's a child for heaven's sake. Any man who takes a child like that should have their manhood cut off.

But he isn't much better.

Sure, he never took advantage of Sunny at the lounge, and he knows she's old enough to make her own decisions, but some of those dancing girls seem so young, and he never questioned their ages, never asked them if they needed help. Dancing isn't prostitution, but it isn't too far off for some women, and the lure of the money is strong. Desperation makes people do things they wouldn't normally, and a better man wouldn't have been a part of that scene.

Law shakes his head to clear his mind. That's all in the past, and this job will soon be done, and Rosie's sister will be safe.

Now he needs to scan the surrounding woods for his hiding spot, go find a room at the inn in the next town up, and then he'll return tonight to start his watch for Rosie.

Chapter Eight

One Day Till Rosie dies

The late morning sunlight streams in the hospital window, and the smell of the sweet pea bouquet invigorates Rosie as she stretches her aching back. She spent the night in this chair holding tight to the grandmother she loves, singing beloved tunes, and listening to Nana's stories of her childhood and all the years she had with the husband she so loved and missed.

Rosie lifts her head off the bed and takes in Nana's quiet body. Nana's chest no longer rises and falls under the thin blanket, her lips no longer twitch as they did last night when she slept. Although her face is so peaceful, so still, Rosie's heart breaks.

Tears flood her face, and she grasps her grandmother's frail hand. "Goodbye, Nana."

She lays a small kiss on Nana's delicate cheek. There are so many things that must be done, but this is the last time Rosie will be alone with Nana, and she doesn't want to give that up. This woman loved her, cared for her, and appreciated her, and now Nana is with the husband she missed. She is happy and free from her pain.

A while later the nurse arrives, and Rosie tells her what happened. The nurse quietly drapes a white sheet over Nana's body. "Would you like some more time with her?" she asks.

"No, thank you. I've said my goodbyes." And now she must gather the pieces of her shattered heart. It doesn't matter how many times she tells herself Nana's death may be for the best, her pain will take a long time to heal.

At least she got to say goodbye to the woman who was more of a mother than Rosie's own mom. She doesn't even want to think about what would've happened if Law hadn't given her a ride. She wouldn't have been able to say goodbye.

The nurse sets a hand on Rosie's shoulder. "Your grandmother was a wonderful patient. We all appreciated her smiles and positive attitude."

"Thank you." The words are not a surprise. Grandmother always was a lively woman, looking for the bright side of life.

"Why don't you come to the office to do some paperwork. Your grandmother left something for you."

KILLING ROSIE

Rosie says one last goodbye and trudges to the small office on the second floor. She hardly pays attention to the words the hospital administrator is saying. He's so cold, sitting there in his dark suit and stiff gray shirt, like dealing with death is nothing, but maybe it is to him. He probably sees it on a daily basis, but a little compassion would be nice.

If Law were here with her, he'd comfort her, hold her, but he's half a day closer to his new life in Stilla.

She's never needed a man, but now she wants one. A man like Law. Strong and confident, but not a dolt or a beast. There are too few like him out there.

All those days at the lounge, she knew he was different. He listened to her with interest and even remembered things she told him.

But he is gone and will likely never return.

"Just sign here, and here," the man behind the desk says. Rosie plucks the pencil away, feeling his eyes on her. She looks up to find him staring at her breasts, and he doesn't even notice she's caught him.

Rosie sighs. Law would probably knock this guy out for being disrespectful.

But Law isn't here.

She forces away the thoughts and signs the papers.

Late afternoon, Rosie finally reaches Radda, the walk from Lakare torturous. She has so many questions about Nana's illness and what was stated in the will. She feels pride for knowing her grandmother trusted her with such a special gift but also knows the disharmony it will cause in the family.

Her face brightens as she passes the Haake's bright red barn, where she and her sisters played with the Haake children. Farther on, the woman sweeping the front porch of the general store waves at her, but it is not Mrs. Norgaard. Perhaps there is a new owner.

All Rosie wants to do is return to Nana's house, but she must stop and see Tindra first. Nana's best friend has been by her side for years, both of them losing the loves of their lives too early.

She approaches Tindra's grand house slowly, the tears filling her eyes once again. Her grandmother is gone, and she feels so alone. Even this home that Rosie often visited when she was younger offers little comfort. But she trudges up Tindra's front steps anyway. The old woman answers the door and smiles.

"Rosie, how wonderful to see you." She wraps Rosie in her warm embrace, smelling of fresh baked sweets.

"Hello," Rosie sniffs and steps back.

KILLING ROSIE

Tindra reaches for the glasses hanging around her neck. Her smile falls, and her face shows no surprise. "Oh dear, I'm sorry."

She pulls Rosie to her once again, and the tears fill Rosie's eyes, the sobs escaping her mouth. Even Tindra knew things were so bad.

Tindra rubs her shoulders, murmuring soft, soothing sounds, and once the crying lessens, she leads Rosie into her parlor and to the sofa. They sit together, and Tindra grasps Rosie's hand with her own withered pale one. "Your grandmother loved you so much. You made her proud."

Rosie wipes her wet cheek and stares at the lacing on her boots. Those words were always the last thing Nana said to her whether it was on a visit or in a letter. It was more than her mother ever did.

"I don't understand why nobody told us how sick she was." Rosie's voice trembles, and she tries to steady it.

"Your mother knew, but your grandmother didn't want to worry you. She knows you would've dropped everything to help her."

Tindra pats Rosie's hand. "I'm sure she's looking down on you with your grandfather right now, telling you to wipe your tears. She is happy and healthy again."

"I know." But Rosie would, selfishly, rather have her grandmother here.

"I was at the hospital a few days ago, and she knew it was coming. We sat and talked for hours until the nurse finally kicked me out. Did you get to see her?"

Rosie looks into Tindra's blue eyes and smiles. "Yes, they let me stay in her room overnight." Those last moments with Nana will remain in her heart forever.

Tindra pats Rosie on the leg. "Let me get some tea going, and we can talk some more."

Rosie waits quietly in the parlor. Her grandmother spent a lot of time here, drinking tea and talking with her closest friend.

Soon Tindra returns with a platter containing two cups and two dessert plates. Rosie's mouth waters. The tea sits on the end table to cool, and Rosie takes a bite of the kladdkaka. The rich and gooey chocolate cake melts in her mouth, and she lets out a sigh.

"Your grandmother's recipe." Tindra grins at her and wolfs down another bite. "Perhaps I would be slimmer if it wasn't for Marta."

Rosie chuckles. "But then you'd miss out on delicious treats as such." The kladdkaka was one of Nana's favorites.

"Very true." Tindra's bright eyes twinkle.

KILLING ROSIE

As Rosie enjoys the cake and tea, Tindra shares a few stories of Nana, and Rosie does in turn. Nana revealed a few stories last night of her younger years growing up with Tindra and the troubles they found, and the memories brighten Tindra's face even more. Rosie can only wish to have such a friend as Tindra throughout her life.

Once their second cup of tea is finished, Tindra stands and shuffles over to her secretary and picks up a cherrywood box. She returns to the sofa and opens it, showing the multitude of folded letters inside. "I'm sure you have some questions about why your grandmother left her home to you instead of your mother."

"You know about that?"

"Yes, dear. Despite the things you'll read in here, your grandmother struggled with her decision, and we spoke often about it. She made the decision just before she went into the hospital." Tindra takes a deep breath and continues. "I'm not sure if you're aware, but some businessmen wanted to buy the land your grandmother's house is on. They offered her an exorbitant amount, but she refused. She didn't want to leave the home that meant so much to her."

"But why?" Nana's lands extend far into the woods—they used to play in them as children, run around playing tag and hide-and-seek. Pappy even built them a treehouse out back.

"They wanted to build a big animal farm and clear out a lot of the trees. Your grandmother spent her whole married life in that house, and she wasn't able to give up the memories. Those years you lived with her after your father died were always strong in her heart."

"What kind of animals?" A memory creeps into Rosie's mind, her mother and sisters talking about selling Nana's house. They had to have known.

"Hogs. And the Balstads and Grendahls were not too happy either, some of the buildings being awfully close to their homes." Tindra stares off towards her window in thought for a few moments. "It doesn't matter anyway because they decided to go with another site farther out of town."

Mother had to know about the offer. There's no other reason they'd talk of selling Nana's home.

Rosie takes the first paper on top. Her name is on it, but the others have no names. Tindra places her hand over Rosie's. "You are meant to read these in private, but if you want someone to talk to, I'm here for you. I've heard it all from your grandmother, so nothing will shock me now."

KILLING ROSIE

She wants to read them at Nana's, alone, so she places the first letter back in the box and closes it. She's never seen the box before but can tell that it's old.

"I'll give you a ride home. If you need anything, you let me know. You may have some visitors though. Your grandmother was much loved."

"I know," Rosie chokes out, her eyes wet again. Nana grew up in Radda and never left; her friendships here ran deep.

They go out to the barn, and Rosie helps hitch up Tindra's horses to her wagon, and very soon she is at Nana's long drive, staring down the dirt road. The house comes into view, and she stops Tindra, who gives her one more hug before she climbs out.

Tindra drives away, and Rosie is alone, staring at the small home at the end of the drive. An invisible hand holds her back, and she hopes maybe that this still isn't real, but it is.

Nana is gone.

Rosie trudges closer to the house but veers into the small clearing in front of the house to the birch tree. Years ago, Nana and Pappy planted four birch trees, one off each corner of their home, in honor of their grandchildren.

She tugs at that graying bark, and it tears off. The trees are not as big as the surrounding woods, but it still towers over her. The curled paper crumbles in her hand, and she blows the pieces off. They silently float to the ground.

"I'm sorry, Nana. I won't do it again," she says aloud. Nana always admonished them for removing the bark.

She leaves the birch tree and enters the house, taking a deep breath. Another wave of tears hits her as she looks around the lonely home.

This is now her house, and hers alone. Nana left almost everything in her possession to Rosie, all of it laid out in a will, which the administrator assured her is legal. Nana didn't have much, but now it all belongs to Rosie, besides the few special things Nana left for Nellie.

Rosie sits on the red quilt her grandmother made in honor of her fiftieth anniversary with Pappy. The room smells like her, of tea and baked goods, and of a life well lived.

So many memories play out in Rosie's head, and she climbs under Nana's quilt to rest her weary limbs, breathing in the smell she loves so much. She soon falls asleep.

KILLING ROSIE

Rosie accompanies yet another visitor to the door and hopes for a bit of quiet. She hasn't had a chance to read the letters, but now is the time.

She takes the cherry box and settles on the sofa with one of Nana's blankets wrapped around her. Slowly, she removes the first letter with her name on it in Nana's handwriting.

Dearest Rosie,

I know you're wanting to ask me so many questions now that I'm gone. But I just wasn't strong enough to talk to you about this in person. My heart aches over the things my daughter has done, and I just can't bear to speak of it aloud to you. But you will see from the other letters in the box one of the reasons why I've made the decision I did.

Those letters are only a small part of my decision though. The biggest reason is you, my wonderful granddaughter, the woman you've become. This house is special to me, and nobody else will love it as you will, and I want you to have it.

I just want you to know that I love you and how much I appreciate you. You and Nellie mean more to me than anything, and I need you to tell her that too.

Love, Nana

Rosie wipes the tears once again, her chest tight, and finishes the letter. There's so many, and she doesn't want to read the words that will cause her more pain.

But she has to.

She opens the first letter, from her mother to Nana. It's filled with complaints because Nana is not sending enough money to support the four grandchildren. The next letter contains many of the same. Rosie had been unaware that her grandmother was helping support them. In fact, Mother had claimed to be sending some of Rosie's money off to Nana.

Rosie reads the third letter, which begins with a vile insult to her grandmother.

You're lying. Don't you know how important it is for your granddaughters to attend school? Linn wants to go to beauty school and Stina wants to be a nurse. How can you take away their dreams? You have plenty of money.

Their dreams? Stina and Linn have never expressed an interest in attending school. Their only interest lies in finding rich men who will take care of them and give them a nice home. Why would Mother say they wanted to go to school?

KILLING ROSIE

Rosie continues reading the letters, wishing she could see the ones that Nana wrote, but it's clear whom the spoiled brat is: her mother.

The next few letters go on with the complaints, and then Rosie gasps.

She re-reads the paragraph.

If you'd sell the house and the land to those men, then we'd have plenty of money. You're selfish. That house means a lot to me too, but selling it would mean a lot more to your granddaughters. To poor Nellie, who is teased at school for her worn clothes.

It's just a house after all and you're a stingy old woman.

The room closes in around Rosie, the way her mother talked to Nana, the cruel words, none of them true. Nellie doesn't wear worn clothes, and she isn't teased at school. Her sisters have no desire to go to school. And Nana... she was so generous and loving. Maybe she had little money to give, but she gave her time and her talents to those around her.

This is just so hard to believe, but the proof is right here in her mother's handwriting. She knew of the businessmen's offer, and she wanted the money for herself, wanted to ship Nana away to some home for somebody else to care for her.

It's almost too much to take, but Rosie has to finish. There's only two letters left.

She unfolds the second to last paper, smoothing it on her lap. She can't help but notice how the letter from a few weeks ago is addressed to *Marta* instead of *Mother*. She's also quite aware of how rarely Rosie's name appears in the letters. It's all about Stina and Linn and Nellie and the things they all want and need. Rosie's name only appears when there's a complaint to be made.

Marta,

Don't you dare. I have been a good daughter. I have done everything you asked of me over the years, and you dare disown me? Father would be ashamed of you. He worked hard all his life, and now you're not willing to leave us what is owned us when you die. So much of that house is mine, and you know how much it'd mean to me and the girls to be able to move up to Radda and live there.

Rosie almost laughs. There's no way her mother and sisters would move to Nana's. Even though the house is in fair condition, and Nana has acres and acres of land, it's half the size of their current home, and Radda is too tiny of a town for Stina and Linn.

KILLING ROSIE

I am done with you. Rosie may be coming to visit you, but I no longer have a mother. I can assure you though that when you are gone, I will get that house. And we will sell it to those business men.

The realization hits Rosie like an angry bull. It's about the money and moving the family to Staden and living amongst the wealthy. It was always *only* about the money. Mother cared not one bit for the mother who tried to love her.

Perhaps Nana died of a broken heart.

Rosie doesn't want to read any more, but there's one letter left, and she picks it up. Nellie's name is on the front though, so Rosie leaves it folded and sets it in the red cherry box with all the others.

As if this isn't hard enough, now she has to go back and explain to her mother and sisters about the will, and she can only imagine all the arguments and blame that they will fling at her. They won't believe her when she says the businessmen don't want it anymore.

Maybe to make life easier, she should just let her mother have the house.

Rosie has so many of her own dreams. Owning her own flower shop or nursery, a house with happy children, a man who loves her. Being in Radda would provide that separation her grandmother so appreciated, but Rosie isn't sure she can be that far away from Nellie. Her sister needs her too.

In a perfect world, Mother would let Nellie live here with Rosie, but that'll never happen. And Rosie will need to find replacement jobs in Radda, which would be more difficult, but not impossible.

Her dreams feel so unattainable, so unrealistic, and she doesn't want to think about it all anymore. Her head is heavy with all this new information, and she just wants to forget it all for a while.

Someone knocks at the door and calls her name. Hugga Ved, the man who often looks in on her grandmother and does the tasks her grandmother could no longer do. Cutting wood and clearing snow in the winters.

Rosie hurries to the door, glad for a short reprieve from all the thoughts flooding her mind.

Chapter Nine

One day Till Rosie dies

Law arrives in Radda in early evening to check on his target. His heart skips a beat at the open red and white curtains on the windows. Rosie is there. He is too far in the trees to get a view of her through the window though, and soon some people arrive. He slides to the grassy ground under the old aspen tree and shifts until he finds a comfortable spot.

He watches and waits. He has until the middle of the night before he'll sneak into the house, so he has a while.

Several people come and go. Too bad he can't get closer to the house so he can hear them, but he doesn't want to risk being caught. Rosie always stands just within the doorway, and he can't get a decent look at her.

Some women bring dishes of food that will never be eaten. A shame.

Law's stomach rumbles, and he digs into the food he brought.

Finally, as the sun is setting, the last visitor leaves.

The final hours tick down, and he replays all the stories in his head that Stina and Linn told him. The awful plan for the brothel. The time Rosie broke her mother's arm. Or even the time she was so mad, she stuck her sister's fingers on the hot stove. The girl screamed in pain until Stina and Linn found her and brought her to the hospital.

Law shudders. All of his targets deserved to die for the atrocious sins they committed, and Rosie belongs in the group with the others. Now Law will be able to provide Rosie's family justice for her evil deeds.

Should he be the one handing out justice though? It's an idea he sometimes considers, but not for too long because if he thinks too hard, he'll know the right answer.

These people like Rosie are monsters, and somebody has to stop them.

Yes, tonight is the night. He hasn't had enough time to watch Rosie like he usually does with his targets, learn their habits and schedules, but this house lies alone in the woods with no witnesses roaming the streets. Nobody will hear a thing.

KILLING ROSIE

Law's mind wanders to Sunny, hoping her grandmother is okay. Law never knew his grandparents, doesn't know where they live or if they're even alive. His mother never had nice things to say about them, and he doesn't even know their names.

Sunny had been so concerned about her poor grandmother. What would she say if she knew what Law was about to do, how he's sitting outside this woman's house plotting Rosie's death? He'd have to explain to her what Rosie has done, but Sunny would not approve.

No. That man tried to kidnap Sunny, and she hadn't wanted Law to go looking for him. Sunny would say he must go to the sheriff, that Rosie belongs in jail.

He mentally slaps himself for letting his doubts seep in. It doesn't happen often, but maybe they're here because this is his last job. Rosie's crimes would disgust Sunny, but she would advocate talking to the sheriff, not doling out his own brand of justice.

But he's ridding the world of one more depraved monster.

The light inside stays on for over an hour after nightfall, and he waits. One hour. Then two. And a third. The whispering trees and chirping bugs of the forest are the only things keeping him company, and he is still wide awake despite the deep dark night.

The light has been off for a while, and now is time to slip into the house. He creeps out of the trees towards the silent house. Only the bugs will be the witnesses to his justice.

Slowly, he opens the door and steps inside. His check earlier showed no creaky floors, so for that he is thankful. Just to be careful, he does a search of the house to make sure there is nobody else, but only two bodies are here. Him and Rosie.

Satisfied, he returns to the bedroom where Rosie sleeps, facing the wall under that red and white quilt. This job is too easy. With his hands he'll take her life before she even has time to wake up.

But a nagging doubt resurfaces along with the image of Sunny in his head.

Beautiful, smart Sunny. He can see the horror on her face if she knew the truth about him. No matter how many times he's tried to fool himself into thinking his actions are right, he knows they are wrong. But he's never really felt like he has a choice. He's needed to justify the first life he took out of revenge.

But there's always a choice. Maybe the sheriff in Radda is different from Staden. Maybe the judges can't be bought off. Maybe they'd care about a little girl being forced into prostitution.

KILLING ROSIE

He could wait until tomorrow when Rosie leaves and burn down this house. Yes, it'll only delay her plans, but maybe he can help the girl another way.

He can't change his past, but his future is his choice. He wants to start clean, and walking away from this job is the way. The money can be returned, and he can retreat to Stilla. It's not like those nutty sisters will know how to find him.

It's what must be done. He may not have Sunny, but he can keep his humanity.

"It's your lucky day," he whispers.

"Who's there?" a quavering voice responds.

Oh no. Think fast. Okay—he's got a story. He's drunk and stumbled into the wrong house.

"It's just me, John." Every village has a John. Rosie flips over in bed, and he can see her face for the first time in the moonlight. Every muscle in his body freezes tight. It can't be…

"Law, what are you doing here?" she says meekly.

His mouth drops to the floor along with his stomach. "Sunny?" He falls to his knees. What is going on?

Sunny is Rosie.

Rosie is Sunny.

He almost killed Sunny.

The bile rises up his throat, and he clenches his hands to keep from throwing up. Innocent, perfect Sunny. He'd almost wrapped his hands around her neck and squeezed the life out of her.

His breaths come short, his face scorching. He almost took the life of this amazing woman.

"Law, what's going on? Why are you here?" she asks. He gazes up to see the tenderness in her eyes. "Did you hear about Nana?"

"Your grandmother? No." What does her grandmother have to do with this?

She yanks him to his feet towards the bed. They sit side by side just staring at each other on top of that red quilt that her grandmother probably made.

All their conversations in the wagon about her family, even the superficial ones in the lounge before he knew her. Sunny is not the woman the sisters described. She would never do what they said. She loves her little sister.

Sunny... Rosie is innocent.

Never once has he regretted what he's done, but suddenly everything is different, and the possibility that there was some other innocent like Sunny whose life he ended hits him.

She stares at him waiting for an explanation, and he has none. His mind is a blank except for one thing.

KILLING ROSIE

He has to tell her the truth. He owes her that, and even if she hates him forever, she can at least make herself safe from the sisters who want her dead.

"I don't know how to say this." Law's eyes close. He's not sure how to say the words, how to explain he almost killed her, that her sisters are monsters and want her dead.

Sunny draws back. "I won't like this, will I?"

No, that's not her name.

"No, Rosie, you won't."

She gasps. "How did you know my name? I... I... never told you."

Law rubs the back of his tense neck and unclenches his jaw. She will never forgive him, but he has to do the right thing, if just this one time.

"It's a long story, but I promise you, I'll never hurt you."

Her face twists from confusion to dismay. "What do—" She shakes her head and slides off the bed. "I think I need to make some tea."

Rosie pads off towards the kitchen, but Law doesn't move. No matter what he says, her heart will break. Her body will fill with fear for what her sisters might still do, and the hatred she'll have for him... That'll be the worst.

He deserves it though. He's no better than that man who attacked her at Uppehall.

Law waits until he hears the whistle of the teapot before leaving the bedroom. Rosie sits at the table with a plate of crackers and two cups.

He sits.

He stares at the cup, the clock on the wall ticking ahead second by second.

Maybe the tea will moisten his dry throat, help him to spit out the story. Law grabs the cup, but Rosie lays her hand on his wrist.

"It's not ready yet, a few more minutes."

"Oh." His tongue ties itself up in knots. "I don't really drink tea." Here they are, a woman who just saved him from drinking tea that's not strong enough yet, and he was about to kill her because he believed the sisters' lies.

"Maybe I should've poured us a few shots of whiskey, but Nana wasn't a drinker." She sighs and stares off towards the hallway.

"Is she still in the hospital?"

Rosie's face falls, tears gathering in her eyes. "She died not long after I arrived. Her poor body couldn't hold out any longer. I'm so overwhelmed. Her friends have been so helpful, so wonderful to me, but I haven't even had a chance to tell Mother." A slight grimace falls across her face, but she pushes it away. "She needs to be here. And my sisters, the twins. And Nellie too." She swipes her hand across her wet cheeks.

Linn. Stina.

The lump inside his throat grows. This can't be happening. Life was so easy before Sunny, and now…

"That's what I need to talk to you about. Stina and Linn."

She bites on her lip. She never told him those names either.

Chapter Ten

Today Rosie dies

"How do you know Stina and Linn?" Rosie tries to process everything that has happened, but it's impossible. She's exhausted and overwhelmed and so, so confused. This night can't get any stranger. Nana is gone, and Law shows up in her house unannounced. She should be scared, but she isn't.

Law sips from his red tea cup and frowns, then looks at the floor, towards the dark window, everywhere but at her. Rosie takes a cracker and chews the tasteless morsel.

"I don't know how to tell you this, so I'll just say it. I'm not who you think I am. Everything about retiring to Stilla is true, but I'm not leaving a job in sales. Your sisters hired me to um… get rid of you."

Rosie spits out her cracker in laughter. "Is this a practical joke? Did they pay you to do this?" Nellie has to be in on this farce. Stina and Linn would never think of such a story, but Nellie... she's the silly one in the family.

Law's face remains grim. No quirk of his lips, no teasing in his eyes.

"Stina and Linn paid me money to kill you," Law says, his voice flat.

Rosie's body tightens, her throat closing. The leftover cracker in her mouth becomes a hard lump. His face is so solemn, so sad, and her body suddenly feels heavy.

A sip of hot tea moistens the cracker, allowing her to swallow. She can feel Law's eyes on her, but she can't face him. Why would her sisters want her dead? They've never got along, and yes, they've treated her badly, but wanting to kill her? And is her mother all a part of this?

"My job was to take care of Rosie. You've got to believe me when I say, I only get rid of bad people. People who deserve to die."

"I've..." Rosie can hardly think straight. Law was about to kill her.

"They lied. They told me you were the one who hurt your mother. That they worried for your younger sister's life. That you beat them. That you were bringing your sister here to open up a brothel."

"With Nellie? They told you I was forcing my sister into prostitution?" She gulps, tears in her eyes, and stands, then drifts over to the window to slide the threadbare curtains aside. The night is black outside.

This can't be true.

"Was my mother involved?" She can't even fathom the thought, of a mother wanting to kill her own child, but then again, she never would've thought that of her sisters either.

But they know about the house, the businessmen. Mother knew Nana disowned her. Which meant she knew the house and land would go to Rosie.

An exorbitant amount Tindra had said. An exorbitant amount her mother wanted.

"I don't know. They never mentioned your mother."

It shouldn't be possible.

But it is. It's quite likely actually. So many things are making sense, conversations with her mother and sisters about Nana and the house.

Strong hands grip her shoulders, and Rosie shrinks away. "Why didn't you kill me?"

Law stands behind her, the heat from his body burning into her. "Because of you. And not because I found out it was you. I was sitting here in the dark, and I imagined the look on your face when you found out

KILLING ROSIE

what I did for a living. I just couldn't disappoint you. I know it's stupid because we hardly know each other, but that's why. I was about to leave, but then you woke up."

Rosie turns around, still trapped by Law's thick arms, his scruffy face inches from hers. She searches the creases around his eyes for lies, for something to say he's wrong, but all she feels is the truth. But it can't be. Her sisters are mean and nasty, but killers?

No.

But their love of money is so strong, and their hatred of Rosie is fierce.

"My sisters wouldn't do such a thing." Even as she says the words, she doesn't believe them. Or more so she doesn't want to believe them.

"I can prove it to you. I have a map they drew for me, but I'll ask them for more money. Then we can go to the sheriff."

"But they'll arrest you too?" He deserves to be arrested, but some part of her doesn't want to see that happen.

"I should be in jail for the things I've done, but I'm worried about you. About what they might do if they're not locked up. Something might happen to you, and we can't risk it. I'll go tell the sheriff right now what I've done if it keeps you safe. If it keeps Nellie safe."

So many tears she's shed these last few days, and now more bubble up. "You'd go to jail for me?"

"Yes." He nods gravely.

The gratitude wells inside Rosie. Nobody has ever done anything so selfless for her before, and maybe she shouldn't have feelings for Law, but she does.

He saved her. If it had been another man, she would be dead. She collapses in his arms, letting the sobs overtake her body. All the pain her mother's inflicted, her sisters, the grief over her grandmother dying, everything spills out onto Law, and he holds her, nuzzles his nose into her head until the tears slow.

She pulls back, wiping her cheeks. Law grasps her chin and tilts it up towards him. "You tell me what you want to do."

"I don't know," she hiccups. Her sisters might try again. And what about Nellie? She's only fourteen, but they already treat her awful. Their jealousy and bitterness will only get worse.

Rosie slows her breathing and tries to sort out all her thoughts. "I need some time to figure out what to do."

"I understand. I'll give you a few days, and then you can let me know what you want to do. I wasn't lying before. I really think you should go to the sheriff."

"I don't know…"

She just needs to think. She has an idea of what she needs to do, but she isn't sure she can say goodbye to this home she's loved for so long.

Law steps back. "I have a room at the inn. I'll return in a few days."

Rosie grips Law's wrist. "Don't leave me. I can't be alone."

His lips press together, and he shakes his head. "But I almost… I mean I was about to—"

"No. You would never hurt me. I know that."

Law's face remains taut, his lips twitching. She knows there's so much turmoil inside him, the bad things he's done, but he's good.

She knows he is.

"I need you," she says.

"Then I'll stay." Law hauls Rosie into his arms and doesn't let go.

Chapter Eleven
No more Rosie

"Are you sure this is what you want to do?" Law asks Rosie one more time.

She glances around the room they rented at the inn and nods. Law doesn't want to leave her, but he must return to Radda to do the job alone. She can't risk being seen.

"Yes, you need to go now. I'll be fine." Her lips press into a tight line. He isn't worried for her safety, but for her emotional health. He tried to talk her out of her plan, but she has made up her mind.

They say their goodbyes, and Law takes off on horseback to get to Rosie's grandmother's house. The trip takes a while, and most of the houses he passes along the way are quiet at this late hour.

After arriving, he gives Misty something to eat and drink and hikes one more mile to the house. The door is unlocked, and he slips inside. Most of the furniture and belongings remain in the house, but Rosie took those things most important to her. He had to remove a few items from his wagon to make room, but those things are not important to him.

Law takes the jug of petro and splashes it across the floor and walls, the smell quickly overpowering the room. He's confident the fire will spread, overtake the house, and burn it down before anyone arrives. But to be safe, he lights several small fires in every room.

The flames swiftly spread, the acrid smell hitting his nose, but Law waits, hiding in the shadows of the trees.

Nobody comes.

The burning inferno doesn't take long to consume the small house, and Law decides it's time to go. He hikes back to his horse to start the journey back to Rosie.

Chapter Twelve

Day one of a new life

Law doesn't seem to believe Rosie when she says she's okay, but she is. She is at peace with her decision to destroy Grandmother's home and keep it out of her mother's and sisters' hands. Faking her death is what needs to be done.

It will only take another two days or so before news of the fire reaches her mother and sisters, so they have no time to wait.

The grief of some of her former friends over her death may be real, but her family… they just love her for her money.

Nellie is the exception and the one worry Rosie has. She doesn't dare consider the possibility that Nellie won't leave with them.

She re-reads through the letter to her sisters. A letter that is written just as much to her mother as it is them.

KILLING ROSIE

Stina and Linn,

I know what you two have done, and I have proof. I've thought long and hard about what I will do. I don't want to go to the sheriff. I don't want to put Nellie through even more pain, so I have decided to let it go.

Everybody will believe I died in the fire, and that is what I want. It is up to you to keep the secret, but if you do not, the whole truth will be exposed, and the sheriff will be informed of what you and Mr. Wolf planned.

I am leaving, moving far away, and I am taking Nellie with me. You can show this letter to Mother, who I know was involved. And tell her that Nana told the businessmen she wouldn't take their offer. They have moved onto another location, and the deal is no longer valid.

Your hearts are dark, and that is why I'm taking Nellie. Don't look for us, because if you do, the truth will be revealed to all.

Your sister, Rosie

A tear drips onto the paper beneath her name, and Rosie smears it away. She won't tell Nellie the full truth, at least not until she's older, but at some point, that day will come.

Rosie sneaks through her old house, the memories now tainted by the acts of her sisters. This house never held much love, and Rosie won't miss it one bit.

Everybody is gone, and she sits on her former bed and allows the tears to fall.

Soon it'll be time to pick up Nellie, so Rosie lays the letter on her sisters' bed. She packs a bag full of Nellie's clothes and grabs a few other special items that belong to Nellie, the things that can't be left behind.

On the front porch she lets the front door slam on her old life, hoping the choices she is making are the right ones.

At Nellie's school, Rosie sits outside to wait. The bell rings, and chattering school children race out of the building. Nellie's laughing face soon appears but darkens when she spots Rosie at Law's wagon.

"What's wrong? Why are you here?" Nellie's frown deepens.

"Nothing's wrong, but we need to talk." Rosie leads Nellie closer to the waiting wagon. "Nellie, I'd like you to meet Law. I'm moving away with him, far away, and we want you to come with. Nobody knows where we're going, and I don't plan on ever seeing Mother or our sisters again. It's your choice on whether to stay or go, and I will respect your wishes no matter what they are, but I dearly hope you will go with us."

KILLING ROSIE

Rosie holds her breath, praying that Nellie chooses to go with them.

They have enough time that if she says no, they can return to the house and replace the letters with new ones, but Rosie can't bear to think that might happen.

"You want me to leave Mother?" Her gaze jumps from Rosie to Law, then to the wagon. "And I wouldn't see you ever again if I stay?"

"Yes, I want you to go with us more than anything. Leaving you would be the hardest thing I've ever done, but…" Rosie swallows the lump in her throat, unable to tell Nellie the truth. "It's a long story, but we don't have time for that now. You just need to trust me and Law."

"What about Nana?"

Rosie steels herself. Somehow with everything going on, she has not prepared herself to break this news to Nellie. The pain in her heart expands.

She grasps Nellie's hands. "Nana died just after I got the hospital, but I got to spend the night with her. We sang together, and she shared stories about Pappy and when we were little kids. And she told me how much she loves you, and she left a letter for you to read."

Tears fill Nellie's eyes. "Really? She's gone?"

Rosie nods and then stares at the man who saved her, after almost killing her. The man who loves her.

"Please come with us." She squeezes Nellie's hands and waits.

"Of course I'll go with you." Nellie throws her arms around Rosie's shoulders, and Rosie sighs with relief. Her sister will be safe, and they will have a chance at a new life far, far away.

Law helps Nellie and Rosie into the wagon, and as they leave town, Rosie closes her eyes, vowing to never look back.

The End

Acknowledgments

Thanks to Lara Schiffbauer for her help in making this story stronger. And thank you to Theresa Paolo who is always there to offer advice with a cover or blurb or whatever I need. You both are super awesome!

Thanks also to those of you who are reading my books. I've finally got some of my work out in this world, and it's awesome to see that dream come true.

About the Author

Reading has always been a big part of Suzi's life. She even won the most-pages-read award a few times in her junior high English class, many years ago. She started several writing projects as a kid but never actually finished anything, and then she took a big break from writing that lasted well into adulthood.

She writes in a variety of genres, including horror, suspense, and women's fiction, and she has even dipped into fantasy slightly with her fairy tale retellings. She also writes young adult novels under the name Suzi Drew.

Her non-writing life includes her family and friends, her sweet and fluffy dog, and an awesome job editing with CookieLynn Publishing. (Oh wait, that's still a part of writing. Seems she can't get away from the written word!)

To find out more about Suzi,
go to SuziWieland.com.

Also by Suzi Wieland

<u>Thriller Novels</u>
Black Diamond Dogs

<u>Horror Novels</u>
House of Desire

<u>Horror and Suspense Novellas/Short Stories</u>
Shallow Depths
(Un)lucky Thirteen
Long-Term Effects
The Silent Treatment
A Story to Tell
Panne Dora Pass

Twisted Twins Series
Glenda and Gus
Two for the Price of One
A Hard Split

<u>Fairy Tale Novellas</u>
The Down the Twisted Path Series
The Whole Story
An Unwanted Life
Killing Rosie
The Perfect Meal
When the Forest Cries
In the Queen's Dark Light

Please visit SuziWieland.com
for more information.

Milton Keynes UK
Ingram Content Group UK Ltd.
UKHW030951261124
451585UK00001B/46